# THE CLUTTER CORPSE

## Simon Brett

CRÈME de la CRIME

This first world edition published 2020
in Great Britain and the USA by
Crème de la Crime an imprint of
SEVERN HOUSE PUBLISHERS LTD of
Eardley House, 4 Uxbridge Street, London W8 7SY.
Trade paperback edition first published
in Great Britain and the USA 2020 by
SEVERN HOUSE PUBLISHERS LTD.

British Library Cataloguing in Publication Data
A CIP catalogue record for this title is available from the British Library.

ISBN-13: 978-1-78029-124-6 (cased)
ISBN-13: 978-1-78029-684-5 (trade paper)
ISBN-13: 978-1-4483-0409-7 (e-book)

All Severn House titles are printed on acid-free paper.

Severn House Publishers support the Forest Stewardship Council™ [FSC™],
the leading international forest certification organisation.
All our titles that are printed on FSC certified paper carry the FSC logo.

MIX
Paper from
responsible sources
FSC      FSC® C013056

Typeset by Palimpsest Book Production Ltd.,
Falkirk, Stirlingshire, Scotland.
Printed and bound in Great Britain by
TJ Books Limited, Padstow, Cornwall.

To Nicky,
The Real Clutter Queen

*'The only normal people are the ones you don't know very well.'*

Joe Ancis

# ONE

I declutter. That's my job. And decluttering takes me into all kinds of areas of human existence. Including crime. Crime like the corpse I found one day.

Most of my work, it has to be said, is more mundane. I tend to deal with a lot of different clients at the same time. I always call them 'clients'. Some people refer to them as my 'cases'. I don't like that. The word has too many medical connotations. Criminal connotations, too. I think using the word 'client' gives them dignity as people. And, to my mind, even the most pitiful of them do have dignity.

My name is Ellen Curtis. I'm old enough to have two grown-up children, and not young enough to have any more. Which in many ways is a blessing. But not in every way. The process of a woman's aging is different from a man's. Perhaps we have more signposts on the road. Perhaps, too, that's why men are so crap at asking for directions.

But getting older doesn't make me melancholy. I am by nature a very positive person. I have had to be.

That particular day started normally for me. My home is a three-bedroomed semi on the northern edge of Chichester, a cathedral city on the south coast. My daughter Jools no longer lives there. She's in London, doing well at the things she wants to do well at. My son Ben spends most of his term times at Nottingham Trent University but, it being April, Easter vacation, he's currently living with me. If he's up when I come downstairs – he quite often is, he doesn't sleep well – I'll offer to make him breakfast. That morning there was no sign of him, so I let him sleep. I didn't even call out a goodbye as I left the house. But I did have to resist the urge to open his bedroom door and check that he was all right. Old habits of motherhood die hard. I remember, when they were tiny, listening at the bedroom door, on the edge of panic, until I heard the reassuring sound of their breathing.

As I passed through the hall, I checked my make-up in the mirror. I don't wear a lot, but if you're dealing with people all day, you've got to look presentable. And if you're likely to be dealing with mess all day, your make-up has to be durable.

The car is always parked directly outside. We don't have a garage where we moved when I downsized, in what I still think of as the 'new' house. Which is daft, because we've been there getting on for eight years.

Before I drove off, I checked the contents of the boot. My car's a Skoda Yeti. It's Pacific Blue and has got my grey SpaceWoman logo below the back window. I wasn't sure about the company name when it was first suggested. Yes, decluttering does involve creating space and, yes, I am a woman. But I thought the name sounded a bit twee. And was it clear what I actually did? Was I raising expectations of astronautical skills, which would be quickly disappointed? Still, it was Ben's suggestion; he was so pleased to have come up with the name that I went along. And it's worked. To change the branding now would lose me a lot of return business.

Underneath the logo on the Yeti, it says, 'Decluttering and Interior Restyling', so that spells things out for the people who might be confused by 'SpaceWoman'. Then there's the website address and my mobile number. I get quite a bit of work from people just seeing the parked Yeti and thinking that maybe they could get something done about their own private glory holes. Some have even contacted me from seeing the car parked outside my front door. So not having a garage in the 'new' house may be a positive advantage. And I prefer it.

I've got the logo and the SpaceWoman name embroidered on the Pacific Blue polo shirts I wear for work. There's something about having a uniform that makes me look more official. I think it may help the clients too. Makes them think their problems are being taken seriously. I do, incidentally, have a great many polo shirts and matching Pacific Blue leggings in my wardrobe. The nature of my work means that at times I get extremely dirty. And, though I'm strongly in favour of recycling, because of the muck I deal with my uniforms sometimes have to be incinerated after only one wearing.

My leggings do have pockets, but I'm too vain about the

outline of my hips to put much in them. One is the occasional resting place for my mobile. In the other I keep a tape measure, because it is amazing how often I need to check available storage space. It goes without saying that the tape measure is not solid and encased in plastic. A folding fabric one in the pocket is much more flattering to my contours. Such vanity.

The kit I keep permanently in the boot of the Yeti consists of heavy-duty black bin bags, a boiler suit, surgical face masks, polythene protective shoe covers and sharp-proof gloves. I buy all such supplies in bulk, but check every morning that the boot's well stocked. I always wear gloves when I first enter a property, though sometimes – to save the occupant from embarrassment – I say it's because I've got a skin condition. Better the guilt should be on me than them. There are plenty of other wrong feet to start off on.

I have a toolbox too. The Stanley knife gets used most. Then screwdrivers, spanners and pliers. It's rarely that the bolt-cutters come out, but hoarders can be – by definition perhaps – extremely protective of their possessions, so I have to be prepared.

I also keep an emergency supply of nappies and incontinence pads, which some of my clients need. And baby wipes. Don't approve of what they do to the environment, but they're so handy.

Then there's a large torch. I rarely work in the evenings, but winter afternoons can get murky. And recesses like understairs cupboards often need illumination.

The remaining boot space is piled high with collapsed cardboard boxes. There's also a plastic container of packs of tape and tape-dispenser guns. I get through those at a rate of knots. They're also the kind of things that can easily get left behind in properties.

Though I say it myself, I am pretty damned quick at assembling a collapsed cardboard box with a tape-dispenser gun. In fact, if it were an Olympic event, I am quietly confident I could make the national team.

The cardboard boxes, incidentally, I get from a greengrocer who has a stall every Saturday in the Cattle Market car park. Like me, he's manic about recycling and happy to supply me with all the containers his fruit and vegetables are delivered in. Better they go to me than to the municipal dump or incinerator.

So, the morning of the day when I found the corpse, having checked out my kit in the back of the Yeti, and having rechecked my Outlook calendar for the appointments ahead, I set off to visit my first client.

For the last few weeks, I've been going to see Queenie virtually daily. If I'm honest with myself, I worry that one day I'll get there and find her dead. But hers wasn't to be the corpse I found that particular day.

As with many of my clients, I was put in touch with Queenie by one of the local housing associations. I have an ongoing relationship with them, and I'm registered with the local authority as a hoarding consultant.

Queenie was in rent arrears, and there had been complaints from residents of nearby flats. I tackled the rent arrears first. She was a slightly other-worldly figure in her early eighties, who had once made a reasonable, if modest, living as a children's book illustrator. But over the years arthritis had so crippled her fingers that she could no longer hold a paintbrush. As a result, she took her state pension and eked out her dwindling savings, unaware of the various grants available to people in her position. I sorted out her financial situation with the local authority pretty quickly. It's something I've had to do many times before.

Dealing with the neighbours' complaints proved more of a problem. Hoarding takes many forms, so do the things hoarded. In Queenie's case it was cats.

The first time I met her in her two-bedroom flat, she had eleven. I'm used to smells – that's a hazard of my trade – but the stench when she finally opened the door to me almost made me gag. In fact, it had been quite strong as I approached along the corridor, so I could understand what had led to the complaints.

It wasn't just inside the flat that the cats offended the neighbours. Queenie's was on the ground floor, and she'd had a cat flap put into one of the sitting-room windows which opened on to the communal gardens. It was the cats' scratching-up of the plants and defecating there that really got up her fellow residents' noses (in every sense).

Like many people with her condition, Queenie just could not see there was a problem. She loved cats. She had always had cats. Some of the most successful books she had illustrated – copies of which she liked to show off to me every time I visited – had featured anthropomorphic feline characters. And though she never voiced the idea, I think that, as a single woman, she had over her life found cats more reliable than men. Or perhaps than people of either gender. She was deeply suspicious of everyone.

Ellen Curtis included. I had to visit every day for a week before she first opened her front door to me. Given the squalor created by her houseguests, Queenie herself was remarkably clean and well-dressed, though worryingly thin. With her private school vowels, she came across as a woman who had slipped downwards from more genteel circumstances. She introduced the cats individually by name, as though they were rare breeds rather than scruffy mogs.

Though I've done courses in Cognitive Behavioural Therapy, I do not claim to be a trained psychiatrist, but in a lot of my work situations I'm dealing with mental health issues. And I recognized from the start that most of Queenie's problems were in her head.

I also recognized that, if I was going to help her, I had to move fast. The other residents of the block wanted her out and, even on that first visit, I could see that sufficient of the housing association's rules had been broken to justify her eviction.

And what would have happened to her then? The chances of Queenie being found alternative accommodation to continue the same way of life were non-existent. She'd be out on her own with all the other local authority misfits, homed in some hostel, B & B, or even a care home. And she'd never see any of the cats again. I had to save her from that.

It wasn't easy, but I have contacts in the RSPCA and various local veterinary practices. (And it's a sad fact that, typically for this country, it's easier to summon help for a distressed animal than it is for a distressed human being.) I took advice and got the same answers from everyone I consulted. The number of cats had to be reduced and, though no one liked recommending the solution, to placate the neighbours, those that remained would have to be kept as house cats. Goodbye, cat flap. Hello, litter tray.

It had taken me more than a month of negotiation with Queenie, but finally she agreed to reduce her total to five cats, all of whom were then neutered and microchipped. The others were rehomed by the vets, and I spent a lot of hours driving Queenie round to see her pets in their new environments. She was still unhappy with being parted from them, but agreed that they had all been allocated to what she called 'nice homes'. Somehow the way she said it echoed the voice of a long-dead mother, who at the end of meals had praised her daughter's 'nice clean plate'.

It was a slow process but, from regarding me as the wicked witch who wanted to destroy everything in her life, Queenie began to trust me.

It was on the basis of that trust that I started my continuing visits. She gave me a spare key; I have keys to a lot of the properties I go to regularly. Queenie I visited partly to ensure that she had emptied the litter trays, which I'm glad to say she usually had. But also to check that she was eating. Though she never failed to stock up with cat food – and lots of other little treats her charges might enjoy – she frequently forgot to shop for herself.

I got into the habit of taking a packet of biscuits with me on my morning visits, making some excuse about having found them at the back of a cupboard. Then, over cups of tea and further viewings of her cat illustrations, I could at least ensure some nourishment passed her lips.

That day, the day I found the corpse, Queenie was more agitated than normal. She didn't go out much, except on her cat-food runs, and wasn't chatty when she did. She had no local network of gossip, she got her news from the television. Didn't bother with the national bulletins – there was nothing in them to interest her – but she never missed the local ones. The presenters held a deep fascination for her. I rarely saw them – out working during the day and usually too tired to catch the 'news where you are' at the end of the evening. But Queenie would still confide in me if a newsreader had got a new hairstyle, or if one of the weather girls was wearing a 'rather revealing outfit'. The local news provided her daily ration of scandal.

Anyway, that morning, before I had even put the kettle on or checked the litter tray, Queenie said, 'Awful business about that woman in Bognor, wasn't it?'

'Sorry, I don't know. What woman in Bognor?'

'It was on the television this morning. She was in a terrible state. You have to ask yourself what kind of monster would do that to her.'

'You mean it was murder?'

'That's how I'd describe it. I'm terrified that kind of thing might happen to me.'

'How had she been killed?' I asked.

Queenie looked at me curiously, as if I were a slow-thinking child. 'It wasn't her who'd been killed. It was her cat.'

'Oh?'

'It's not the first case I've heard about locally. Young people. On drugs probably. You'd have to have a sick mind to torture a cat, wouldn't you?'

'Yes.'

'Still, there are a lot of people with sick minds around these days. Lots of people with mental health,' said Queenie, with the complacency of someone who would never consider that her name might be included in that number.

I was struck, not for the first time, by how many people use the expression 'mental health' to mean the exact opposite.

While I was at Queenie's, the mobile had blipped a couple of times with text messages. I checked them as soon as I got in the Yeti. There's something inside me that means I have to respond to text messages as soon as I get them. Emails too, actually. It could be news of some crisis with one of my clients. Or the family.

The text was family, but not worrying family. My mother. Fleur Bonnier. Once an actress. Still an actress, she would probably argue. Or 'actor', more likely she'd say. She's very obedient to her own code of political correctness. 'One may not work so much these days, dahling,' she would say to me, 'but the instinct to act never dies.' Something which, in her case, I have witnessed on many occasions. To call her a 'drama queen' doesn't come near.

Still, I don't worry about her much now. She's in one of the more stable stages of her life. Married, for the third time, to Kenneth, a solicitor. So, for once, no money worries. And, to add even more to my mother's satisfaction, he's four years younger than she is.

She wasn't even married to my father. He was an actor she'd worked with in *A Streetcar Named Desire*. Fleur assured me it had been an affair of passion – 'All of my affairs have been affairs of passion, dahling.' But I never met him. And when, in my early teens, she told me he had died, I felt absolutely nothing. She was by then married to her first husband, who was perfectly amiable to me, but with whom I felt no bond either. Despite the amount of psychological literature I have read on the subject, I've never been aware of missing a male parental presence in my life.

Fleur, typically, landed me with her surname. Bonnier. Ellen Bonnier. She insisted the name was of Huguenot origin. I never found any proof of that and was very glad to be shot of the name when I got married. So far as I can gather, in my early years, Fleur treated me like a rather daring accessory she had bought. A lot of her theatrical chums apparently described her as being 'very brave' to face life as a single mother. But pretty soon, when a new lover came on the scene, she lost interest in her new accessory.

Fleur's text that morning read: 'Going to the gym at Goodwood. Lunch there afterwards? Say oneish? X F'.

Goodwood is the local stately home, whose estate features a hotel and fitness spa. In the latter my mother spends an inordinate amount of time and money. Kenneth's money, of course. The range of designer gym wear she owns fills a whole wardrobe. She usually fits in her session on the cycling machine or a swim late morning, so that she can stay for lunch. And lunch, for Fleur Bonnier, invariably includes wine.

When she was acting, she was professional enough not to drink until after the evening's theatre show or the end of a day's filming. Now she's not acting, she shows no such restraint. And if I were to join her in the Goodwood restaurant, she would expect me to drink wine with her. I would restrict myself to one small glass – the loss of my licence would end my decluttering career – while Fleur would tank off round West Sussex with half a bottle inside her. Rather annoyingly, she's never been stopped by the police. Her licence is innocent of penalty points (whereas I have got three from some mercy mission I had to do for Ben a couple of years back).

My mother does not take my work seriously. She treats it as if it were some kind of hobby, and her constant invitations for me to go and share boozy lunches with her are an expression of that belief. She knows I'm going to refuse the offer – lunch for me is either a sandwich bolted down in the car between appointments or a meal completely ignored – but she insists on making it. I no longer even reply to those texts.

The second one is from Hilary. One of my closest friends – or perhaps I should say one of my more recent close friends. Working in the same area where I was brought up, I'm still in touch with a lot of girls from school. 'Girls' we call ourselves – who are we fooling? Perhaps I should say 'a lot of women I used to be at school with.' But I've known Hilary for less than ten years.

I met her when I was doing the CBT course. I guess what drew us together was a mutual fascination with what makes people tick. That, and being more or less of an age, and both single at the time. Also, Hilary was one of the less flaky people on the course. Anything in the mental health area attracts its fair share of weirdos, people more concerned with treating their own problems than helping others. Hilary and I were at least serious about the subject.

In fact, so far as the academic side was concerned, she was a lot more serious than I was. I was looking for basic understanding of the therapeutic resources that might be required in my decluttering career. Hilary went to the next level, and indeed a few levels after that. She trained as a psychotherapist at the Tavistock Clinic, and is now fully qualified. She specializes in working with offenders, spends a lot of time in and out of prisons. She is scarily high-powered.

We actually have another connection, too, in that I introduced her to her second husband. Nice guy called Philip Boredean, with whom I had a brief fling when he was a medical student and I was only just out of school. He's now a cardiovascular surgeon, and the relationship with Hilary seems to work fine. No kids, but that doesn't seem to worry either of them. I pride myself on my skills as a fixer, but that's the only time I've ventured into matchmaking. And it wasn't really deliberate on my part. I just introduced the two of them at a party, and they took it from there.

Hilary acknowledged my input by inviting me to be her bridesmaid. I said I would, so long as we changed the job description. I reckoned I was a bit gnarled by then to be called a 'bridesmaid'. And I certainly wasn't going to be a 'maid of honour'. We settled on 'bride's best friend'.

Now I rarely see them together – they live mostly in London – but Hilary is often down south for work. They've got a weekend place, a former coastguard's cottage at West Wittering. It's been modernized and made-over to a very high spec. Though a nineteenth-century coastguard might have found the white-painted exterior familiar, he wouldn't have recognized any of the gleaming steel and glass inside.

Philip and Hilary have a boat at the local yacht club, but it doesn't get used much. He keeps talking about taking more time off, weekends of sailing to take his mind off the stresses of surgery, but such breaks rarely seem to happen. Philip's one of those people for whom work has always had more appeal than leisure.

My friendship with Hilary has survived strongly, though. I'm different with her than I am with other friends. Most of the ones from school I join up with to have a laugh, knock back a few drinks, discuss our lives' triumphs and disasters. Usually the latter. Men, children, boredom, frustration, the unwelcome transformations of age – somehow the problems don't seem so bad when you're surrounded by other people finding the funny side. You may go straight back to reality when you get home, but at least you've had a brief respite.

It's not like that with Hilary. I'm not saying she has no sense of humour – she can be very relaxed and witty – but when we get together, we pretty soon get back to the question that exercises a burning fascination for both of us; what makes people tick?

Though we know each other very well, there are areas of each other's lives that are private. For example, Hilary never talks about her childhood. When the subject first came up, I remember her announcing, 'Oh no, Ellen. You don't want to intrude on private grief.' The words were said in a jokey way, but I'm sure there was some truth in them.

As a result, her childhood was off-limits. That was fine with me. I didn't particularly want to discuss mine. There were other areas of my life I didn't want to talk about either, so we laid down unspoken ground rules. And kept to them. That's one of the advantages of making new friends when you're older. They haven't witnessed your past life, so you can present them with whichever edited version you choose.

Hilary did once mention that she used to go on a lot of creative writing courses, but it was soon clear she didn't want to talk about that either. A passing phase of her life, perhaps, an early ambition which had faded. Again, fine by me. We had plenty of other stuff to talk about. Silences between us were rare.

The text I got from her that morning read: 'In Chichester today. Something I'd like to talk about. Any chance of a coffee at BC?'

'BC' is Buon Caffè, a one-off coffee shop, much nicer than any of the identikit chains. I use it often. That day I had to drive through the centre of town for my next appointment, so I immediately texted Hilary back. 'Could do, so long as it's soon, get tied up later in the day. Nine thirty?'

She pinged back the single word, 'Perfect'.

Hilary is one of those women who's suffered through her life from being beautiful. A problem I've never had, at least not on the scale she's endured it. I've been beautiful enough to the men who have found me beautiful, but never stopped the traffic. Not so for Hilary. She's trim-figured, blonde, and has blue eyes so big that they give the misleading impression she's innocent. For this reason, people – and I suppose I really mean men – have a great problem in taking her seriously.

She tries to counter the danger by dressing in severe dark trousers and high-necked tops, but that seems to make things worse rather than better. She looks as though she's wearing a uniform and, of course, a lot of men have always been turned on by uniforms.

That she could have those looks and also be highly intelligent is something a lot of male brains have difficulty accepting. As a result, Hilary is sometimes over-eager to assert her academic qualifications. Maybe that's why she got them in the first place. That's not a criticism of her. It's an observation. She's also remarkably unaware of the effect she has on men. Particularly young men. On more than one occasion, Hilary's got into awkward situations with young men. When she's been teaching, working with junior colleagues, she doesn't notice how many of them fall head over heels in love with her. With some women, such lack of observation would be an affectation, a way of drawing more attention to herself. Not so Hilary. She is genuinely surprised by each new impassioned declaration.

I'm in Buon Caffè often enough for Giovanni, who runs the place, to know that I'll order a flat white. After that momentary pause that affects all men while they take in her beauty, he asks Hilary what she wants. 'Same, please,' she says.

We do a perfunctory check on each other's home life.

'How's Philip?'

'Oh, as ever. More interested in carving up some other woman's heart than in nurturing mine.' It was said as a joke, but there was a kernel of truth in it. During our brief fling, Philip never left me in any doubt that his studies came first. That was what brought the relationship to a premature end, I suppose. At that age I was more demanding of men, or possibly, as I now recognize, less secure with them. If I had a boyfriend – and Philip was one of my first (after a few fumbling one-night stands) – I wanted his focus to be entirely on me.

But Hilary's words didn't worry me. I knew their marriage really worked. I don't think the lack of children was a cause for regret. They'd never have fitted them into their high-achieving lives.

'Philip's actually going to be down at the cottage this weekend,' she said. 'At least he says he is. And he means it . . . until some medical emergency takes precedence. I was wondering, if you're at a loose end Sunday evening, why not come over and have a drink? Some supper, if you like? Philip always loves to see you.'

'Can I let you know on that? Not certain what Ben's going to be up to that evening.'

'Sure. We're not talking about a dinner party here. Just a drink and fridge leftovers. Let me know.'

'Will do.'

'So, how are the offspring?'

I reported that all was well with Jools and Ben.

'And your mother?'

Raised eyebrows are all I need by way of answer. Hilary knows Fleur Bonnier.

'Anyway, what is it you want to talk about?' I ask. With her I know it won't be frivolous.

'Client I've got . . .' Hilary begins.

Both of us deal with people about whose lives confidentiality is essential, but we both benefit from discussion of the issues we face. So, like most professionals in our kind of world, we've developed work area ground rules. The first of these is: no names.

'Someone from Gradewell?'

Hilary nods. I'm referring to a local open prison. She's doing some research work on the behaviour patterns of lifers. These are convicts who do the last couple of years of their sentences in an open prison, in the hope that, unlike the maximum security places where they've served most of their time, the atmosphere there is more like the real world into which they will shortly be catapulted. If Hilary's in Chichester, it almost definitely means she's working on her Gradewell project.

'Problem?'

'Potential problem. One I'd value your advice on, anyway.'

'Pick my brains,' I say, with a magnanimous wide-handed gesture. 'You're welcome to anything you can find there.'

'Right,' says Hilary, gathering her thoughts for a moment. It's a habit she has, and it results in her always speaking with great concision. 'It's one of my lifers.'

'Thought it might be.' I know that when she says 'lifers', she means 'murderers'.

'He served twelve years in Erlestoke . . .'

'What category's that?' Prisons are graded from 'A', for the really dangerous prisoners, down to 'D' for the most relaxed regimes, like open prisons.

'"B",' Hilary replied. 'And he's serving the last two in Gradewell. He's going to be released in a couple of weeks.'

'And?'

'And the plan was that he was going to move back in with his mother on the Hargood Estate in Portsmouth. Do you know it?'

'I know Portsmouth.'

'Well, the Hargood Estate is the bit of Portsmouth that isn't a "Historic Heritage Site". I'm talking about social housing. Pretty squalid.'

'And you're worried that, in his old environment, he'll get back in with bad company and . . .?'

'It's not that so much.'

'Who did he kill, by the way?'

'His live-in girlfriend.' Hilary sighed. 'The usual thing. It had been rocky between them for some time. Both alcoholics and users. Both with a terrible record of relationships. She had a son who was taken into care a long time before. Ongoing history of police being called out for "domestics". Very well known to the cops in the Worthing area. Anyway, one day an argument between them gets out of hand. He hits the girlfriend over the head with a frying pan. No other suspects. He gets sent down for eighteen years, later reduced to fourteen.'

'Good behaviour?'

'That kind of thing, yes.'

'And what's he like?'

'Like the others,' says Hilary, with a note of resignation in her voice.

She doesn't need to spell this out to me. We've discussed it often enough. Most of the lifers she works with are the saddest and least threatening men you could ever meet. Many are frankly terrified of leaving the rough comforts of prison and going out into a world that has changed for them beyond all recognition. I'm sure somewhere out there are the vengeful psychopaths so beloved of crime writers, but they're probably not the kind to be given two years' acclimatization in Gradewell before release. The really dangerous ones are kept locked away in their Category A prisons for as long as possible.

'So, what's the problem? Is his mother a bad influence?'

'No, I don't think she has an evil bone in her body. It's just . . . well, the circumstances in which she lives.'

I began to see where this was going. 'Are you saying she's a hoarder?'

Hilary nodded glumly. 'That's it. The place should have been checked out before he moved in, but the Prison Service have got such a backlog of work, it didn't happen. Then the flat got inspected last week.'

'By his probation officer?'

'"Offender manager" is the current term.'

'Ah. It would be.' I had long ago stopped trying to second-guess the changing language of officialdom.

'Anyway, the offender manager was deeply unimpressed by what he saw. He says it isn't suitable accommodation for N— for my client.'

'If he didn't go to his mother's place, what would it mean . . .?'

'Going to some dreadful hostel or halfway house or B & B. The kind of place where he definitely would be mixing with just the sort of people he ought to keep clear of. I'm sure he'd be back inside within six months.'

'Though not for murder.'

'Hopefully not for murder.'

'Is the mother happy about the prospect of having her son back?'

'Apparently. I think, apart from the hoarding, she's also losing it a bit. Mind and body, I'm afraid. Not probably long for this life. But my client's very keen that he should go to her place. He wants to make up for neglecting her all the time he's been inside.'

'Have you met her, Hilary?'

'No.'

'So, what's the situation now?'

'I've spoken to the offender manager, who is unfortunately so inundated with work that he can't take any action in the short term. We've got a fortnight.'

'Till your client's released?'

'Yes. A fortnight to get the mother's house into a state that would make it suitable accommodation for him when he is released.'

'OK.'

'And I said that I knew this . . . "person" who's made a career of decluttering. Obviously, the employment of "this person" would have to be cleared with the offender manager – and probably his bosses in the Prison Services. But I think it could make the difference between my client quickly reoffending or actually having a chance to make something of his life.' Hilary brought her face close to mine. 'Will you do it? Check out this house for decluttering?'

'Of course,' I said, sublimely unaware of what I was getting myself into.

# TWO

We left it that Hilary would try to get clearance from the offender manager for my involvement. He was so snowed under, she couldn't say how long it would take. Employing me would also have budgetary implications, and government departments didn't have a great track record for the speedy authorization of payments.

I have, incidentally, long since made it a rule that I never work for nothing, however deserving the cause. My conscience is clear about that, because of the time I spend in follow-ups with clients. For instance, in the case of Queenie, I invoiced the Housing Association for my initial consultations and the time I spent rehoming some of the cats, but my continuing visits, like the one that morning, are unpaid. And I have quite a raft of former clients on whom I still keep an eye.

Hilary was going to an eleven o'clock lecture at the University of Chichester Criminology Department, where she's doing her PhD, so we parted about ten fifteen. I too had an eleven o'clock appointment. I said that, in the unlikely event of Hilary getting clearance from the offender manager that day, I could juggle my diary to get to the Hargood Estate at the end of the afternoon, say about five.

I mentioned that I deal with a lot of different clients at the same time, and the next person on my list could not have been more different from Queenie.

I could have told that from the address, apart from anything else. The house was a substantial Edwardian property in the leafy suburbs, on the way out of Chichester if you're travelling west, in an area where there are quite a lot of big houses. This one was called 'Clovelly', a town somewhere in Devon, I recall. The house wasn't in great decorative nick, but it was big. Price? Definitely talking seven figures.

The call had come from a woman called Dorothy Lechlade.

She was making contact secretly, which is not unusual in my line of business. And she gave me more information than might be expected in a first conversation with someone she hadn't met before. Again, that is not unusual in my line of business. In a precise, slightly old-fashioned voice, she told me that her husband was an historian by profession (she actually said 'an'). Theirs had been a late marriage, he in his mid-sixties, she in her early fifties. Remarkably in this day and age, the first time for both of them. She said that, since each had been living on their own for a long time, there were many adjustments to be made. Many compromises required. People become set in their ways and the introduction of someone else into a single existence almost inevitably prompts discussion, if not outright disagreement.

She hastened to assure me, as if I was about to question it, that theirs was a very happy marriage. However, she was worried that the rooms at the top of the house in which Tobias worked were in need of some reorganization. Was that the kind of service I might provide?

I had assured her that it was. I told her my charges. Her response suggested that money was not something she had ever had to worry about. I then suggested that I should make a preliminary visit, a recce to assess the scale of the job. I asked if she thought it would be better if I met husband and wife together for that meeting.

This idea unsettled her and she got very fluttery as she chose the option of my seeing her for the first time when her husband was out. She was elaborately secretive as we fixed the date. Tobias Lechlade, by long habit, spent Fridays in London, researching at the British Library. He always caught the same trains to Victoria and back. If I were to arrive at eleven in the morning, he would be safely absent. She gave me her mobile number and said she would ring mine if we needed to change our plans – if, say, Tobias was ill on the appointed day. Belt and braces.

The big deal Dorothy Lechlade made of all these arrangements suggested that she was inexperienced in the ways of duplicity.

So did her reaction when I parked the Yeti outside the house at two minutes to eleven. She had clearly been watching for me and scurried straight out and asked if I'd mind parking a little further down the road. She didn't want to advertise to the good folk of Chichester that she required the services of SpaceWoman. It was not the first time I had encountered that reaction. Dorothy Lechlade was a tall woman with greying hair cut in a long bob. My mother would have described her as 'handsome' or have said she had 'strong features', both of which in the Fleur Bonnier lexicon meant 'unattractive'. I found her rather appealing. I also, in a strange way, seemed to recognize her from somewhere.

She wore a grey pinafore dress over a navy-blue shirt and I was not surprised to hear that she had until recently been head of history at a local girls' private school. Before that, she insisted on telling me, she'd trained as a social worker. 'Thought, you know, having come from a very privileged background, I should do something to help people less fortunate than myself.'

Her first job had been in Worthing, but she'd found dealing with abandoned children 'very distressing'. 'So many of them just get lost in the care system, it's heartbreaking. I'm afraid I wasn't up to that kind of emotional stress. Some of the cases were really harrowing . . . toddlers whose parents had died in violent circumstances. I'd always said I'd wanted to work with children, but I just couldn't handle that stuff. I didn't have the required ability to shut my mind to it when I got home. I'd wake up from nightmares about the kids. I was in a bad way.' She winced with the pain of recollection.

'So, I gave it up and retrained as a teacher. That was a more suitable role, in which I could still be of some use to children.'

Her manner was strange. She combined practicality with a slight other-worldliness.

I accepted her offer of coffee and followed her through to the kitchen while she made it. She used an all-glass Cona Percolator, an antiquated device I hadn't seen for a long time in these days of Nespressos and pods. Looking round the brown-painted space, I got the feeling it wasn't the only thing that had stayed there unchanged for many decades. I felt certain that she had moved into her husband's house, rather than the other way round.

As if detecting the direction of my thoughts, Dorothy said, 'Tobias's parents lived here, since before he was born. He wasn't actually born in the house; women went to nursing homes to have their babies in those days. Funny, isn't it: then a "nursing home" was for having babies, now it's for the very old.'

She was talking too much, betraying her nervousness. I did not interrupt.

'But he's lived here all his life so, you know, he's quite resistant to change.'

I began to see the scale of the difficulties she might be encountering.

She poured the coffee. I said I was happy with cold milk. It came out of a high cream-coloured fridge with a bulging front, another vintage item.

'Would you like to drink it down here?'

'No. Let's go up and see where the problem is,' I suggested, tactfully ignoring the fact that the problem might well pervade the whole house. This impression was reinforced as she led me up two flights of stairs to the top floor. While well on the right side of squalid – and believe me, I know squalid – the décor was in need of a little refurbishment. Wallpaper, featuring rather too many large flowers, was faded, scuffed and rubbed at by the passage of the house's residents. The stair carpets were thinning at the edge of the treads.

This should have prepared me for the top floor, but I was still taken aback by what Dorothy's opening of the door – and switching on of the light – revealed. The attic comprised two rooms which, in the days of servants, were probably their living quarters.

The first one was lined with bookcases, full of dusty tomes which might once have had some order but were now stuffed in higgledy-piggledy – upright, sideways, diagonal, upside-down. Many had also cascaded to the floor, where they joined an under-growth of more piled-up books, beige files and loose documents, stained brown where their paper clips had rusted. From the landing door, which could not be opened fully because of the books stacked behind it, a thin path – like an animal track through long grass – led to the second room.

Here the chaos was even more pronounced. The large windows which looked over the street in front were almost obscured by piles of documentation on their sills – I realized why Dorothy had switched the lights on. And, though there were fewer shelves, the tide of books and papers had risen to a couple of foot deep in places.

On the desk in front of the window, only just proud of the surrounding litter, stood a manual typewriter whose natural habitat was a museum. Microsoft might have staged a takeover of the entire world but had achieved no foothold in this attic in Chichester. Even the telephone on the desk was a black Bakelite one, its receiver attached by a plaited brown wire.

And over everything was a sticky patina of dust.

The only item in the room that had been touched by any form of cleaning was a small free-standing bookcase beside the desk. In this stood, erect as guardsmen, a series of books whose spines boasted their authorship by 'T.J. Lechlade'. I took a note of the publisher's name.

Following my eyeline, Dorothy said, with considerable pride, 'Tobias's publications. His special period is the Wars of the Roses.'

'Ah,' I said, not pretending to have any special knowledge of the subject. My recollections from school history lessons were hazy. I knew York and Lancaster were involved, but which side had which rose I'm afraid I couldn't remember. It's one of many things that I've got this far through my life without knowing. And my ignorance doesn't hold me back – the Wars of the Roses don't often come up in my line of business.

'You do see the problem . . .?' said Dorothy tentatively.

She phrased it as a question and the only possible answer was self-evident. I still said, 'Yes.' And then went on, 'But presumably your husband has his own way of working, and it's been like this for years? He knows where everything is?'

I was sounding her out, seeing if my intervention was really needed. Though I couldn't personally have survived more than a few seconds in that environment, I recognized that people are different. And if conducting his life in that level of disorder suited Tobias Lechlade, then who was I to make him change his ways? I don't feel I have a God-given mission to declutter everything. Some hoarders are not doing any harm to anyone and should be left to their own devices.

'Yes,' Dorothy replied. 'But I'm worried from the safety angle. I mean, you can smell it, can't you?'

Funny, I'm so inured to much worse smells that I hadn't really analysed the one in the attic. But now I focused, I was aware of that thick stench of tobacco which used to greet you every time you walked into a pub. I saw on the desk a rack of briar pipes and an ashtray full of ash and dottle.

'You mean the fire risk?' I asked.

'No. The damp.'

I sniffed again and realized what she was talking about. Beneath the predominant pipe tobacco was another fungal layer of smell. Mushroomy, cellar-like.

Dorothy pointed to a corner of the room where – from the top of the wallpaper – there seeped down an uneven black stain. Papers and books had been moved away from the floor beneath, but the damp had darkened the exposed carpet and was clearly spreading.

'Hm,' I said. 'Does it get worse when it rains?' She nodded. 'Then it needs sorting. Have you got a reliable roofer?' She shook her head. 'I could give you a couple of names. Locals. They won't sting you.'

I have a list of such essential people. Roofers, electricians, plumbers, decorators, all of whom I've worked with before. Most of them called Don, Dan or Dean, for no very good reason. I recommend them to private clients. When I'm working for the local authority or a housing association, I have to work with people they approve. Quite a few of my private workmen appear on both lists. There is no better way of finding the right man for a job than word of mouth.

'Oh,' said Dorothy. 'If you could. I'd be so grateful.'

'And while you're getting all that done . . .' I looked around at what looked like an explosion in a paper factory '. . . presumably you'd like me to make a start on this lot?'

'What do you mean?'

'Well, decluttering it.'

'What, you mean . . . *interfering with Tobias's workspace?*' She spoke the words as if I'd suggested painting the Taj Mahal Day-Glo pink.

'Not interfering. Just tidying it up a bit.'

'Tobias wouldn't like that.' She sounded deeply shocked. 'We couldn't do it. It might affect his *work*.'

'You mean you don't want it decluttered?'

'Well . . .'

'Why did you ring me, Dorothy? Why agree to me coming out here? If you just wanted me to recommend a roofer, I could have done that on the phone.'

'Yes . . .'

I could tell she was losing her nerve. I went on, 'Listen, apart from the leaking roof, this place is a major fire hazard. And if your husband smokes up here . . .' The stench of tobacco was now becoming irksome. You quickly forget how it used to permeate virtually every building you walked into.

'But,' said Dorothy feebly, 'Tobias has worked up here all his life.'

'And there's no reason why he shouldn't continue to work up here for the rest of his life. Just work in a rather more organized space.'

'He won't like the idea,' she said.

'Not at first. But he may be persuaded to see the sense of it.'

'I don't know. Tobias is very strong-willed.'

I wondered briefly if she meant he was a bully, but somehow her tone was too affectionate to support that reading. 'Listen, Dorothy, you wouldn't have contacted me if you hadn't considered some level of decluttering up here. I'm happy to undertake the job, but only in consultation with you *and* your husband. From the impression I get of him, Tobias won't like the idea of your going behind his back. If you want to proceed, call me and we'll fix another appointment for me to meet you and Tobias together. If I don't hear from you, I'll know you've changed your mind.'

Dorothy Lechlade seemed to take that on board. As she opened the front door and let some light into the gloomy hall, she asked, 'Oh, what do I owe you for today?'

'Nothing. I don't charge for the first consultation. If you decide you do want to go ahead, then I'll charge you at the rates we discussed.'

'Fine,' she said. 'And thank you.'

I realized, as I walked down the road to the discreetly distant Yeti, what an effort it had cost Dorothy Lechlade to contact me. I also realized that, if their marriage was going to work, she was

going to have to take issue with her husband over other things
that he might not like.

I didn't know whether I would ever hear from her again. The
chances I would have put at exactly fifty-fifty. But I was intrigued
by the Lechlades. I'm naturally curious about people. I couldn't
do this job if I wasn't.

And I felt confident that I could help Dorothy and Tobias, if
they chose to take up my offer. I saw no reason why they couldn't
have a very happy marriage. In spite of everything, I am still by
nature an optimist.

But I knew that, if I did start working at Clovelly, it would
be a long job.

I had heard the ping of an arriving text while I was with Dorothy
and, once in the Yeti, I opened it. From Hilary. 'Contacted the
offender manager and the Housing Association. Both happy for
you to check out the place today. There'll be no one there, the
mother's had to go into hospital, so you'll have to pick up a key
from the Housing Association. Now it's official, I can tell you
the released lifer is called Nate Ogden. His mother's name's
Maureen. I've said you'll visit about five, but since there's no
one there, I guess the exact timing doesn't matter.' She gave me
the address of the flat on Portsmouth's Hargood Estate and the
landline number there.

The intervening hours were filled like most of my days are.
A wasted journey to Arundel, where a brother and sister in their
fifties wanted their late mother's house emptied as quickly as
possible so that they could get it on the market and realize their
inheritance. I had made it clear to them on the phone that I do
decluttering rather than house clearance but, like many people,
they just hadn't listened. I gave them the contacts for a couple
of house clearance companies I know to be reliable. They didn't
even thank me or apologize for wasting my time. I got the
impression, from the simmering atmosphere between them, that
they couldn't wait till they were once again alone to argue about
the terms of their mother's will.

Lunch was a chicken and sweetcorn wrap eaten hastily (and
almost definitely illegally) while I was driving back along the coast
to Smalting to visit one of my former clients in a care home. She

was a widow whom I had helped downsize from the family home to a two-bedroomed flat, and then helped to choose which few belongings she could take to the small room which was now the extent of her property. She had a daughter in Australia and a son in New York, neither of whom had visiting their mother in West Sussex high on their priority list, and most of her contemporary friends had died. So, I had got into the habit of visiting her at least once a fortnight. I never felt I could stay for less than half an hour. That, I suppose, is another bit of the job that I do for free.

My next call was in Bognor Regis, not the posh bit of holiday brochures and genteel retirement flats. Like most seaside towns, Bognor has an underbelly of unemployment, deprivation and drug abuse. My client there was a girl called Ashleigh. Because of an alcoholic mother, she had spent most of her childhood in care. And before she was eighteen, she had given birth to a little boy called Zak. Though a father was never mentioned, the child's appearance showed him to be mixed race.

I had been put in touch with Ashleigh by the local authority. They had found her a one-bedroomed flat but were worried about how she was coping there. As ever, neighbours could be relied on to raise objections to any new tenant, though whether their complaints were justified, or born of resentment at the idea of a single mother getting preferential treatment, it was hard to know. Many times in my work I'd heard grumblings about 'these girls who just get deliberately pregnant and rely on our taxes to pay for their housing.'

I had visited a couple of times, and on each occasion been struck by how much Ashleigh adored Zak. He was the light of her life, the first thing that she had ever felt genuinely belonged to her. If motherhood consisted only of hugging her baby, Ashleigh would have been wonderful at it.

Sadly, though, in the more practical aspects of the job description, her shortcomings were all too apparent. As is common with girls like her, Ashleigh didn't want to breastfeed. And when it came to preparing Zak's formula food, her schedule was fairly random.

She was equally erratic in nappy-changing. Having never experienced any kind of nurturing from her own mother, she had no instinct for it. In the same way, having never eaten much home cooking, she lived on takeaways. And, presumably, when Zak was weaned off the formula, he would be put on the same diet.

Ashleigh also seemed to see no reason why having a baby should stop her from going out drinking with her girlfriends. I hoped that it stopped at drinking. She had certainly used drugs in the past. I prayed that she was through that stage in her life.

The reason I'd been called in was because of the limited resources of the social services. They simply hadn't got the staff to follow up on a case like Ashleigh's. So, they reasoned, if they could reclassify her problem as hoarding rather than general inability to cope, they could get in an outside contractor – i.e. SpaceWoman – to deal with it. Employing me every now and then was a lot cheaper than taking on the new permanent staff members they really needed. They were up against it with the funding cuts in the sector.

Their version of events was true, in a way. There was a decluttering problem. Ashleigh had a chronic inability to tidy anything up. Each time I visited, the floor of her flat would be littered with empty packs of formula and spilled powder, dirty nappies, damp sheets and fast-food cartons. It was as if she genuinely didn't notice the chaos around her. Every time I had to point it out for her to become aware of the mess. Then she would make half-hearted attempts to tidy up, but I would end up doing most of the work. My supply of black bin liners, and indeed clean nappies, would be raided every time.

It took me a long time to understand Ashleigh. She was certainly not uncaring – she adored Zak – but she didn't seem to understand the basic practicalities of care. And what worried me was that if she didn't get a grip on her life, if she didn't stop living in self-generated squalor, the council would have her out of the flat in no time. If – heaven forbid – she started on the drugs again, Zak would definitely be taken into care. In that event, the chances of her ever getting him back were pretty slender. The cycle would be perpetuated.

So, the challenge to me was to convert her undoubted love for her son into the form of caring for him properly.

When I arrived at Ashleigh's that afternoon, she was playing music too loudly. Some version of rap – perhaps the latest subdivision of the genre that I hadn't caught up with yet (and probably never would). Though I didn't mention the noise right away – didn't want to come across too much as the disapproving mother – I knew it was just the kind of thing to generate more complaints from the neighbours. But I think playing music too loud, just like the squalor in which she lived, was something Ashleigh just didn't think about.

Zak still looked beautiful, through the encrustations of formula and snot on his face, but he was screaming. The causes were a nappy that hadn't been changed for too long, and sheer hunger. I pointed them out to Ashleigh.

'Yeah, I know. I've just never been very good with time, knowing when things need to be done, you know.'

The easy route would have been for me to change Zak's nappy and mix his formula – as I had done on earlier visits – but I saw my task as building Ashleigh's self-reliance. So, I monitored her through the necessary processes. She was far from incompetent. She changed the nappy efficiently, cleaning his little bottom up with baby wipes (my baby wipes). As she did so, I noticed there was a bit of redness about his tiny anus, the beginnings of a rash.

'You'd better put some cream on that.'

'Oh.' Ashleigh looked at me hopelessly. 'I haven't got any cream.'

Another thing to add to the list for my next visit. Sudocrem.

The contents of his nappy had leaked on to his Babygro, to join other noxious substances there. I picked it up gingerly. 'For the washing machine,' I said.

'Washing machine's buggered,' said Ashleigh.

'For how long?' She shrugged. The pile of filthy clothes in front of it suggested at least a week.

'Have you rung the Housing Association about it?' I knew the terms of her rental agreement. The washing machine was their responsibility, not hers.

She shrugged.

'Why not?'

She shrugged again. I made a mental note to call the Housing Association.

Holding Zak on her hip, Ashleigh riffled though the clothes in front of the washing machine and found a Babygro slightly less soiled than the others. She put it on him.

She brought the same efficiency that she had to the nappy to mixing Zak's formula. While she did it, I was allowed to cuddle him on my lap. Which I knew was a big concession to me. Ashleigh was very wary of letting anyone else touch her baby – something which had raised another problem with health visitors and got the words 'difficult and uncooperative' indelibly imprinted on her notes. She was one of those people who always, often unwittingly, managed to get on the wrong side of officialdom.

While she prepared the mixture, she kept giving little, covert looks in my direction. To check I wasn't doing Zak any harm. When the bottle was ready, she almost snatched him from my arms. She settled down to feed him, holding him close, almost making me feel I was an intruder in this moment of mother/son bonding.

Zak seemed restless, so I suggested gently that the level of music might be putting him off.

'Oh, I'd forgotten that was still on.' She sounded as if she really had. Mercifully, she used a zapper to extinguish the sound.

After its changing, Zak's dirty nappy had just been dropped on the floor and lay next to a Kentucky Fried Chicken box spilling over with gnawed bones. I looked around the small space. 'Where're the nappy disposal bags?'

'Mm?' asked Ashleigh, unwilling to have the feeding togetherness interrupted.

'When I last came, I brought you some nappy disposal bags, to put the dirty ones in.'

'Oh, I think they're over there.' She gestured towards a pile of debris by the sink.

I found them. The packet was unopened. The nappies on the floor must have been all the ones used since my last visit. And if Zak had been changed with the frequency that he should have been, there could have been twice as many of them.

Deliberately, I opened the packet of nappy bags, rolled up the nappy Ashleigh had just changed, put it in the bag and tied the handles. 'That's what needs to be done with all of these,' I said.

'Oh well, if you don't mind . . .'

'I do mind. You clear them all up when you've finished feeding him.'

Ashleigh's face assumed a very put-upon expression, but she didn't raise any objection. I knew I was using a very mild form of tough love, but I did somehow have to get her to take responsibility for her own life. And Zak's. It was the only way they were going to survive together.

Reluctantly, Ashleigh handed him over to me again after she'd finished feeding. With a baby wipe I removed the excess from his face, and he snuggled into my chest, comatose. As Zak slowly twitched against me, the inevitable, atavistic memory came back to me of cuddling Juliet (before she became Jools) and Ben in the same way.

I did not have to give Ashleigh any further instructions. She picked up and folded each reeking nappy into a bag and tied it up. She put them in the black bin liner I had provided. Then she picked up all the discarded formula boxes and fast-food containers. They went into the bin bag too. The carpet they revealed was stained and here and there dusted with formula powder.

Finally, she got out a vacuum cleaner and swept over the floor. The room was transformed. The actual cleaning process had taken less than twenty minutes.

That was what was so frustrating about Ashleigh. She knew exactly what she should be doing. It was actually doing it that was the problem.

My next visit was another waste of time. I didn't recognize the name or address on my Outlook calendar, but that didn't surprise me. Bookings come at me from all kinds of sources – the SpaceWoman website, phone calls, texts, and sometimes quite a long way ahead. I'm perhaps not as organized as I should be about my diary. I tend to work a week in advance. If there's a name I don't recognize, then I can guarantee it's a first consultation. And quite often those get aborted. People approaching me about their own problem have cold feet. People approaching me about a family member's problem get worried about the family member's likely reaction to my appearance. Usually, they contact me to cancel. I never attempt to dissuade them. That's the decision they've made and, fortunately, I don't have to look for more work.

The one that afternoon was annoying, because they hadn't been in touch. And the address was way into the Downs beyond

Goodwood. The satnav directed me towards a dusty, little-used track. By the entrance from the main road hung from one rusty hook a faded sign reading 'Walnut Farm'.

When I reached my destination, the old farm building looked as if it had been uninhabited for years, but I have learned in my work not to judge by appearances. Many hoarders are as careless about the exteriors of their homes as they are about the over-crammed interiors.

Pressing the bell push, tapping on windows, banging on front and back doors, none of them had any effect. The place was locked up and felt it had been that way for a long time. So, I put the excursion down to experience. If the clients got back to me, I might ask about the missed appointment. If they didn't, I wouldn't bother.

I didn't hang about. I had to move on.

As arranged, I picked up the key from the Housing Association and, though Hilary's text had said it didn't matter what time I arrived, it was, as per schedule, just after five when the Yeti drew up outside the block of flats on Portsmouth's Hargood Estate.

It had started to rain on the way, which meant there were few people on the streets, and the relentless grey drizzle didn't add to the charms of the area. Everything was extremely run down. Road pockmarked with potholes, cars whose smashed wind-screens suggested they'd been there for a long time. Inevitable plastic bags and McDonald's wrappers in the gutters. The area around the entrance to the block was graffiti-covered and smelt of uncleared rubbish.

I knew that Portsmouth had undergone considerable urban redevelopment in recent years. Well, the process hadn't reached the Hargood Estate.

I put on my sharp-proof gloves – you never know what you're going to encounter in a new site – and walked into block. In the enclosed space of the entrance hall, the rotting smell was intensi-fied and new graffiti had covered the old. The lift, it goes without saying, did not work.

I still saw no one. Perhaps it was the rain, or perhaps the residents were afraid to leave their flats.

The people at the Housing Association had told me my destin-ation was on the second floor, so I climbed up to it. The concrete stairs were wet. There was a sound of dripping. The rain was getting in somewhere.

All of the flat doors were blue, though the paint was stained and flaky. I stopped outside 27. The once-shiny brass numbers were dull and tarnished. There was a bell. I pressed it, but no sound came from inside. I knocked tentatively on the door with my knuckles, then harder a couple of times. Still no response.

I wasn't expecting a reply, but I had to go through the routine. Maureen Ogden, Hilary had told me, was in hospital. I wondered what for. Serious hoarders do not like leaving their premises, nor do they like to let strangers in. I've been doing what I do long enough to know that they are very secretive. They may not see anything strange about their obsessions, but they certainly don't want the results to be observed by people they don't know – or, in many cases, by people they do know.

I used the key the Housing Association had given me and, the minute I stepped inside, recognized the smell of the hoarder's home. Much stronger than the whiff of the stairwell. Dust, paper, wool, damp, with various less appealing undertones.

The pathway through the hall, narrowed down by teetering piles of cardboard boxes, told me the same story. Though I'd brought my torch with me, I switched on the light.

Five doors led off the hall, two either side, one at the end; all were closed. The one straight ahead opened on to the kitchen. Or half opened, I should say. The clutter behind the door saw to that. Access to the stove and sink was just about possible, though the fridge could not have been opened until the stepladder and ironing board propped against it had been moved.

But, rather as with the copies of Tobias Lechlade's books, there was an oasis of tidiness in the midst of chaos. The kitchen table's surface was covered in small rectangles of paper and cardboard, neatly held in blocks by rubber bands. A closer look showed me that they were all coupons, the kind of coupons which mostly come in free local magazines – granting free pizzas, discount dog food, '50p off your next purchase of granola bars', '25% off a main course on production of this coupon', 'A free 175ml glass of house wine, red or white, with any steak ordered', 'Kids Eat Free', and hundreds of other offers that sounded too good to be true (and usually were).

There was a system to the way the coupons had been categorized. Restaurant offers in one pile, food shopping in another, discounts on clothes with their own section and so on.

It was a phenomenon I had frequently noticed with hoarders. There is one area of their life where complete order reigns. By focusing on that particular special interest and seeing that that's in order, they can genuinely make themselves unaware of the surrounding shambles.

One end of the table seemed to be reserved for scratch cards. Used scratch cards. Maureen Ogden's hoarding instinct didn't allow her to throw any away. Next to the scratch cards was a pile of coupons offering large prizes, tens of thousands of pounds in what were described as 'Giant Cash Draws!' (each one decorated with an exclamation mark). Maureen Ogden was clearly a woman dedicated to augmenting her pension. Whether any of her attempts to win a fortune had been successful, there was no way of knowing.

I went back into the hall and had a real problem opening the second door. My job involves a lot of heavy lifting, so I'm pretty fit – gym membership at Goodwood would be a waste of money for me – but there was something so heavy propped against the inside of this door that for a moment I didn't think I'd make it.

I tried one final shoulder-charge, however, and that did the trick. I heard a crashing sound as something I'd dislodged fell away, and was able to push the door wide enough to squeeze my way in.

The space, presumably designed as a sitting room, was not large but it was piled high, floor to ceiling, with furniture. Furniture of all kinds: armchairs, office chairs, tables, cupboards. The item which had fallen over to allow me access to the room was a tall Edwardian coat stand, with a series of pegs round a central mirror. Heaped up higher than me in the centre of this nest of wood was a pile of bed clothes. Not modern, duvet-style bed clothes. Old knitted blankets, discoloured pillows, eiderdowns covered with material that looked like silk but wasn't.

As I looked down, I noticed one unexpected item sticking out of the wall of bedding.

It was a human hand.

# THREE

Afterwards, I was asked by the police why I had touched anything at a crime scene. The answer I gave then – and the answer I'd still give now – was that I didn't *know* it was a crime scene. My first instinct on seeing someone injured is to try to help them. And I didn't immediately realize that the hand I saw belonged to someone dead.

I shoved aside the old blankets and eiderdowns on top until the body was revealed. A young woman, difficult to say exactly how old, probably somewhere in her early thirties.

And dead. I'd suspected that from the stiffness with which her hand had poked out from under the bedding, but a touch confirmed it. The emaciated, tattooed body was cold and dry.

In moving the bedding, I had dislodged an empty syringe, which had fallen from a couple of layers above the corpse. Her arms were a battleground of perforations, and there was a wisp of blood from one, probably the most recent needle mark, probably the one that had killed her.

Any hope that she might have been the victim of an accidental overdose, though, that she had for some reason been rooting around in the bedding and dislodged a pile which had fallen and trapped her, was quickly snuffed out. There was the syringe, for a start. Unless she had injected herself, covered herself with bedding and then placed the syringe on the blankets above her, someone else must have done that.

Besides, her face was swollen with bruising, and on her wrists were marks where something thin, and probably plastic, had been used to tie them together.

A tangle of black-dyed hair thickened with dried blood suggested the possibility that the overdose wasn't the cause of death, that she might have died from a head wound.

All I could think of were Hilary's words, how Nate Ogden had killed his live-in girlfriend. 'He hit her over the head with a frying pan.'

But I knew I was allowing my mind to move too fast. The only verifiable fact I now had was that I was at a crime scene. And when you're at a crime scene, the first thing you do is ring the police. Which is what I did.

But I did something else before that.

There were still three rooms I hadn't been in. Two of the doors were closed, one was ajar. The door next to the sitting room opened on to the bathroom. The bath itself was so full of dusty boxes that it clearly hadn't been used for a long time. Narrow passages through the debris ended at the toilet and the washbasin. The latter was the only place where any washing had been done for a while.

The other closed door was opposite as I came out of the bathroom. Also over-crammed with stuff, but here some attempt had been made to make the space more liveable. There was more order to the piles of boxes, as if they had been stacked up recently. Space had been created around the single bed. It actually had a duvet, which had been straightened and smoothed down. On a bedside table was a clock radio, also a tin of roll-up tobacco and a packet of Rizla papers. It looked like the habitat of someone trained in the disciplines of prison.

I didn't think I was leaping to conclusions by reckoning that it was Nate Ogden's room. Maybe in the run-up to his release, he'd had some days out when he'd been allowed to visit his mother and prepare the space where he would be living.

I closed the door behind me, as I had done with the bathroom, and moved to the one that was ajar. I had to pick my way gingerly between the clutter, almost toppling it over at one point.

I assumed this was Maureen Ogden's room. It had a sour old woman smell. But even if she had been in there asleep and not at the hospital, it would have taken me some time to find her. The space was so full of furniture, blankets and magazines that the bed had no recognizable outline.

I went back to the kitchen to ring the police and wait for them.

If they remained unaware that I'd visited all the rooms in the house, then that was fine by me.

They arrived within ten minutes, a Panda car, two male officers in uniform. When I showed them what I had found in the sitting room, their reaction showed that murders were way above their pay grade. One of them got straight on to his phone, presumably to summon specialist support. The other asked if I'd mind stepping downstairs into their car to answer a few questions. They didn't want to contaminate the crime scene more than was necessary.

In the car, rain still drummed on the roof and slid down the windows. The young man was very uneasy. 'I just need to get a few basic facts about you. I'm sure there'll be more detailed questions when the others get here.' His tone suggested he hoped the 'others' got here soon. He didn't like murders. He'd rather be back dealing with handbag snatches in Gunwharf Quays shopping centre.

After a cursory check round the flat, the second officer came and sat in the Panda. He had locked the place up with the keys I had been given. He seemed less anxious for the 'others' to arrive soon. Maybe had ambitions in the direction of detective work. His colleague was happy for him to take over the questioner's role.

Their first assumption was that I must have lived in the block, and it took a while for me to persuade them that I had nothing to do with the Ogdens. I pointed to my brand-marked Yeti parked in front of them as validation of my profession.

The aspiring detective then asked if I'd been in any other rooms apart from the kitchen and the sitting room. So, the one detail I'd hoped to keep quiet didn't stay quiet for long. But there was no point in lying. In my experience, it always gets you into worse trouble.

Of course, it struck me, my questioners knew as little as I did. Probably less. Being a policeman on patrol must be a little like being a GP – you never know what problem you will be dealing with next. It could be a brawl in a pub car park, a slashed tyre, some old biddy who's locked herself outside her house, or a child snatched in a supermarket. The cops have to be prepared for anything and get as much basic information about the situation as quickly as they can.

So, though I found their questioning slow and tedious, I remained very amenable. They were only doing their job. Besides, I needed time to process what I had seen in the sitting room.

The 'others', the specialist support arrived, in the form of a male and a female officer. They wore plain clothes and came in an unmarked car. Having asked the two uniforms what was to be expected inside the house, they donned white protective suits and face masks before entering the block.

It felt like an achingly long wait before they re-emerged. By then it was well after six thirty. I asked permission to text Ben. I'd told him the night before I'd be home in time to cook supper. There was now no chance of that.

In the course of the next half-hour, the two police cars had been joined by a parade of other vehicles, from which more white-clad figures emerged. The sight of a single Panda was probably not uncommon on the Hargood Estate, but this cluster of cars and vans left no doubt that there had been a major incident. The rain had stopped by then, people started to emerge. Curious local children – and not just children – were ushered away, and soon the police had ringed the area with tapes attached to plastic bollards. It would only be a matter of time before the press arrived.

Now the experts were there, the two uniforms couldn't wait to leave. They passed me over to a plain-clothes Detective Sergeant, whose name I instantly forgot, and the Panda sped away. It struck me I hadn't got the names of the two uniforms either. Strange, I'm normally good with names. It must have been the shock getting to me.

The detective sergeant led me to a van equipped with seats and a table. 'If you don't mind waiting here, madam. We'll be with you as soon as we can.'

As he left the van, he had a whispered word with a female officer with a yellow hi-vis gilet over her uniform. Her job seemed to be keeping the snoopers of the Hargood Estate at bay, but I got the clear impression that she was also on guard to see I didn't make a run for it.

That was not something I was about to do. But the wait did seem interminable. Sitting down allowed the week's exhaustion to catch up with me. I longed to be back at home, a bottle of Merlot open, sitting opposite Ben, eating the meal I'd just cooked for us.

He hadn't responded to my text. Funny, he usually did, even

if it was about something trivial. Another anxiety to add to my general unease.

It was pushing nine o'clock by the time they got round to me. A tall, weary male officer, and a shorter female. Both in plain clothes, dark suits, looking like office wear. Neither with a wedding ring, and the woman had no other jewellery either. Nor make-up. I don't know why I always notice such details, but I do. Other details I'm not so good at – or I wasn't that evening. They introduced themselves, but again – a sign of my stress – the names didn't register. He was a detective inspector, she a detective sergeant. Perfunctory apologies for keeping me waiting. They gave the impression that keeping someone waiting when you're starting out on a murder investigation is a minor detail. And I could see their point.

Basic questions about who I was, where I lived, what I did for a living. Not very difficult to answer.

And then they got on to the more detailed stuff. What was my relationship with the Ogdens? Did I recognize the murder victim?

They seemed to keep circling round these points, rephrasing the questions slightly but still reverting to the same subjects. Their approach wasn't exactly adversarial, but I began to wonder how I would respond to it if I were guilty, if I *did* have anything to hide. And I didn't. The one piece of information I'd considered keeping secret, the fact that I'd explored the rest of the flat, I had already revealed to the uniforms in the Panda.

And yet I couldn't lose a residual feeling of guilt, the kind one used to feel, regardless of one's innocence, in the presence of a headmistress.

The detail that seemed to obsess the police was why I had come to the flat on the Hargood Estate. I explained exhaustively what my job was, but they still didn't get it. I told them how the visit had been arranged by Hilary through the Housing Association and gave them their contact details. That didn't seem to help. They went back to asking me whether I'd ever met Maureen or Nate Ogden. It took a long time for them to accept no as an answer.

By then, it was a quarter to eleven, and they couldn't come up with any reason to detain me longer. The detective inspector did warn me that further questioning might be necessary at a later date. He gave me his card, with numbers to ring, and an email address, in case I remembered anything else that might be relevant to their investigation.

Then he asked me to let them know of any travel plans I might have.

'What, you think I might flee the country?' I asked, to lighten the tone a bit.

My interrogator had no desire for the tone to be lightened. 'It has been known,' he said lugubriously.

Rarely have I been so glad to get back into the Yeti.

I had to concentrate like mad on the journey back to Chichester. I was so exhausted I genuinely worried about falling asleep over the steering wheel. And my worry about not hearing back from Ben grew uncomfortably.

It vanished when I got back, mind you. He was absolutely fine. More than fine, he'd cooked a really nice chilli con carne for me to come home to. And opened a bottle of Merlot.

I thought I'd be too exhausted to eat, but the first glass of wine relaxed me. And Ben was in one of his very chatty, funny moods.

'So, what kept you so late, Ma?' He only calls me 'Ma' when he's feeling good. It's one of those things that started as an affectation, almost a joke, and kind of stuck. But he still always says it in a slightly ironic way, as if he's sending up his usage of the word. 'Fancy man?'

'I should be so lucky. No, it was work.' I didn't elaborate on how I spent the evening. Ben wouldn't have found that odd. I do have a strict confidentiality deal with my clients. I might sometimes speak about a job I'm on in the abstract, mentioning no names, but Ben respects my choice when I don't discuss work.

Besides, thinking about the nastiness of the evening I had just been through, I could never be sure what was likely to upset Ben.

The chilli con carne was excellent. Cooking is just one of many skills Ben has, along with his artistic talent and his empathy with computer technology. And as I sat opposite him, eating the food he'd cooked for me, drinking the wine he'd poured for me, I realized all over again how much I love my son.

And how much I worry about him.

I'm in utter darkness. There's a strap diagonally over my front, hard against my sternum, dividing my breasts. Another is tight across my thighs. I'm anxious and sweaty. I need fresh air. I swallow.

What I breathe feels like air. But it does not refresh like air. I gasp, taking down more of it, hoping that this mouthful will bring the release of oxygen. But it gives me nothing. A dry rasp at the back of my throat, a taste of metal, a tightening sensation behind my eyes. Pain, a gasping, rasping pain, that scours my throat and chokes me with the certainty that I will never breathe again.

I wake in a tangle of sweaty bedclothes. What I thought was a strap across my chest turns out to be a tightened twist of sheet. Even the darkness is no longer utter. The red glow of my clock radio tells me that it is 3.17 a.m. I am not confident of finding sleep again that night. And it's too late to take a Zopiclone. If I do, I'll be even less fit for anything in the morning.

I haven't had the dream for a long time. I dared to believe I'd grown out of it. But, like recurrent depression, it has come back. And like the return of a depression believed to be defeated for good, it leaves me completely without hope. I thought I had made advances in the last nine years. Now I know I haven't.

It must have been the shock of discovering the corpse that brought the dream back that night.

# FOUR

I try not to work weekends. Sometimes impossible to avoid it, but I'm always so knackered by the end of Friday that I need my recharging time. If I don't get a break, I know it'll catch up with me the next week.

Of course, when I say I don't work, I'm referring to SpaceWoman work. The house doesn't keep itself clean and tidy. Nor does the shopping get done automatically. And though Ben could surprise with a spontaneously prepared chilli con carne, his brain isn't wired in a way that might make him check in the fridge to see what essentials need replenishing. Or make him take the next logical step of doing the replenishing.

Anyway, by the time I got up on the Saturday, I felt totally drained. As anticipated, there had been no more sleep after 3.17 a.m. when I woke from the dream.

And the recurrence of the dream had really unsettled me.

No sound from Ben's room. I had the normal dilemma about whether I should open the door while I was on the landing, or call up to him from downstairs, or just go straight out to do the shopping. I opted for silence. But just as I was passing through the hall, my mobile rang.

Hilary. She had heard about the corpse on the Hargood Estate through her contacts at Gradewell. They had rung to warn her they'd given the police her number, because she'd been involved with Nate Ogden in her lifers research. The police, in their turn, had rung and asked if he had ever talked to her about a woman he wanted to get revenge on. Had she ever heard him threaten violence towards anyone?

Through the fuzzy, sleep-deprived haze of my brain, I could recognize that was the obvious question to ask. A murdered woman has just been found in the house of a man who was shortly to be released at the end of a long sentence for murdering a woman. He had recently visited his mother at the house . . .

it's not rocket science. And the police are, generally speaking, better at the obvious than they are at rocket science.

'Did they asked any detail about the research you'd been doing at Gradewell?'

'No, just general stuff. They knew that I'd come into contact with Nate. Asked if I knew where he might be.'

'"Where he might be"? Nate Ogden hasn't been released yet, has he, Hilary? Surely he's still in Gradewell?'

'No. He's gone over the wall. Well, there's not much of a wall to go over there. You just walk out.'

'When was he last seen at Gradewell?'

'Thursday evening. He had a meeting with the governor.'

'About his forthcoming release?'

'No. The governor gave him the news that his mother had been taken into hospital. The Queen Alexandra in Portsmouth. Nate was given permission to go and visit her.'

'Unaccompanied?'

'Yes. He was so near the end of his sentence. He'd had un-accompanied days out to visit her at home before that. And he'd always got back to the prison at the time he was meant to.'

'So, did he go to the hospital?'

'On the Friday morning, yes. Just in time. His mother died round noon.'

'Poor man.'

'But that was the last sighting of him. The guy I spoke to at Gradewell reckoned there was a pretty strong chance that Nate might have gone straight from the Queen Alexandra to his mother's flat.'

'Which would place him there early on the Friday afternoon,' I reasoned.

'Yes. Before you arrived and . . . found what you found.'

'Maybe he found the body first?'

'If he did, all he had to do was call the police.'

'Come on, Hilary, is someone with his history going to call the police? I would think he just panicked.'

'But it's terrible.' There was despair in Hilary's voice. 'To abscond so near the end of his sentence. He's worked so hard to get to this point, and now he's screwed the whole thing up.'

'So why do you reckon he didn't go back to Gradewell?'

'The obvious answer would be because he'd killed the woman you found in his mother's flat.'

'Do you believe that? You think he's likely to have turned violent again?'

'Everything I know about him would make me say no. All right, physically, he's a very strong man and he's not very articulate. He killed a girlfriend with whom his relationship, from the case notes I read, had always been volatile. One day he just lost his rag. A long build-up of anger which he had limited ways of expressing, so he just lashed out. That doesn't make him a psychopath, not someone who gets pleasure out of killing for its own sake.'

'And presumably the victim isn't another of his girlfriends?'

'It seems nobody knows who the victim is yet. But, generally speaking, twelve years in Erlestoke and two in Gradewell are not very conducive to building up new relationships.'

'I can see that . . . though you do read of these cases of women starting to write to men in prison and—'

'There was nothing like that in Nate Ogden's records.'

'OK. I just thought—'

'Really,' Hilary interrupted me again, 'we can't get any further in thinking about the murder until the victim's been identified.'

'True.'

'You found her, Ellen. You'd didn't recognize her or . . .?'

'If I had recognized her, I would have told you straight away. After telling the police, obviously.'

'Yes, of course you would.'

'But, no, her face was horribly bruised and . . .'

'Oh God. And you . . . you're all right?'

'A bit shaken, inevitably. And very tired. I didn't get much sleep last night.'

'The dream? Did the dream come back?'

'No,' I lied instinctively. Hilary was one of my closest friends, and a trained therapist. I had told her about the dream fairly soon after I met her. Once I knew she was someone I could trust. But at that moment I wanted to process recent experiences on my own. 'Anyway, I was just on my way out to the shops, so . . .'

'Sure. And, incidentally, after what's happened, you may well not feel like it, but the offer's still on for tomorrow evening.'

'Tomorrow evening?' I echoed blankly.

'Coming over here for supper.'

'Oh, yes. Sorry, I . . .'

'See how you feel.'

'I'll let you know. Is Philip with you yet?'

'God, no. He was going to drive down this morning but had to rush into the hospital in the small hours. Patient with post-operative problems. Same old story.'

'But you think he will be at the cottage tomorrow?'

'Says he will be.' I could hear her shrug down the phone. 'Anyway, let me know if you hear anything, Ellen. Did the police say they'd need to talk to you again?'

'Yes.'

'If they do share any information with you . . .'

'We are talking about the police here, Hilary,' I said, 'so how likely is that?'


'Are you going to be around for lunch, Ben?' I asked on the Sunday morning.

I knew what the answer would be. It's not that my son doesn't like my mother, it's just that every time they meet, he knows he faces interrogation. She wants to know every detail about what he's doing now and what his plans are for the rest of his life. Also, whether he's got a girlfriend. Inevitably, that takes him into areas he'd rather not discuss.

'Actually, Ma, I'd thought of going for a long walk on the Downs.'

I couldn't argue with that. It was a fine April Sunday. He'd cycle up in the direction of Midhurst to get on to the South Downs Way. He might then walk two hours east, and two hours west, back to where he'd chained up his bike. My son is, physically, a very fit young man. And I've never doubted the therapeutic value of exercise.

'What about food?' I asked.

'I have just had the hugest of All-Day Full Englishes.' The residual smell and the pile of pans in the sink bore witness to the truth of his words.

'Will you be gone before Jools and Fleur arrive?' My mother always insisted on my calling her 'Fleur'. I think it started out because she feared that being called 'Mum' or 'Mummy' in public might make her sound old. Now she thinks it makes us sound like friends, women who enjoy going out and doing girly things together. Which is a gross misreading of our relationship.

'Probably,' Ben replied. Then, automatically, 'Give them my love.'

It used to worry me that my son and daughter didn't get on better, but recently I've become more philosophical about it. Shared DNA is no guarantee of mutual affection, and they can be civilized with each other when they do have to be together. But they are basically very different people.

My firstborn has been tough, unsentimental and acquisitive from the moment of her arrival. I brought Juliet, as she was then, up to be independent, to believe there's nothing a man could do that she couldn't. But I do sometimes worry that I went too far. At what point does 'being your own person' become 'being selfish'? My daughter's independence has hardened into a carapace that seems to shield her permanently from the softer emotions. She knows what she wants and she goes out and gets it.

In this respect, she is of course very like my mother. I have never questioned that Fleur Bonnier has a great deal of charm, but everything she does has to be about her. I know this, to my cost, from my upbringing. During my formative years, her acting career was blooming. That had been Fleur Bonnier's time in the sun, a time which the rest of her working life has never quite replicated. But during those days of success, she was always on the way out: theatre in the evening, filming during the days. And I was always parked with a rolling repertory of nannies, au pairs, not very close schoolfriends and their mildly resentful parents.

As a result, I have no recollection of a nurturing mother. Like Ashleigh, I suppose, though in totally different circumstances. And, I hope, with totally different outcomes. I tried very hard to learn to be nurturing with my two and, though I may have got close with Ben, I don't think I really cracked it with Jools. But perhaps that's partly to do with her personality.

Anyway, Ben having very wisely defected, I was reconciled to it being three generations of women for Sunday lunch. At my place, of course. Though my mother is lavish with invitations to take people out for meals, she rarely invites them to her house. It's not that she can't cook. She honed her culinary skills for arranging tête-à-tête dinners with various men over the years, but that was just another weapon in her sexual armoury. She wouldn't bother to deploy it just for family.

And her relationship with her current husband, Kenneth, has got way beyond trying to impress in that way. Almost all their meals are eaten out.

He will, needless to say, not be with us for Sunday lunch. Sundays for him mean golf. So do Saturdays. And weekdays he's at the office. I sometimes wonder why he bothered to get married. He and Fleur hardly see each other. Which is maybe the best way of maintaining a relationship with my mother.

Over lunch – pork, crackling, all the trimmings; I do a pretty good roast – Jools actually raised the subject of Kenneth's absences. When they talk together, my daughter and mother go into a sort of arch, teasing manner, which I find infuriating. And which they both know I find infuriating.

'So, Fleur . . .' Jools too has always been encouraged to use the first name. Same thing as with me, emphasizing the suggestion that they're girlfriends rather than granddaughter and grand-mother. And obscuring the detail that they're more than fifty years apart in age. 'Is Kenneth making his usual escape from you down at the golf club? I'm surprised you're happy to let him out of your sight for so long. I'm sure there are lots of lascivious lady golfers down there, flaunting their putters at him.'

Fleur grinned complacently. Her make-up was, as ever, perfect. Even after a few glasses of wine – and she'd had three before we sat down – there was never the tiniest smudge to her lipstick. 'I have complete confidence in Kenneth. He knows there's nothing out there that he can't get better at home. He'll always be back at bedtime.' My mother rolled her eyes knowingly. 'You know what men are like.'

She was well aware that I found this acutely embarrassing. Historically, particularly in the post-Freudian world, children never really want to be reminded that their parents have any form of sex life, and in most families the subject is just gracefully avoided. Not with Fleur Bonnier, though. I suppose her sex appeal was always one of her selling points as an actress, and so she had reasons to focus the public eye on it. But to keep bringing it up when she was in her seventies, and to her family was . . . well . . .

Jools of course found it hysterical. Her response was to say, 'Go for it, Fleur!' and ask for more details. Knowing precisely how uncomfortable that was for me.

Jools's words prompted a predictable cycle of innuendo about her grandmother's relationship with Kenneth. 'He tells me a lot of his mates down the golf club are on the Viagra these days. I blame the wives. Kenneth's never had any difficulty in that department. You know, if there were more women in the world like me, the makers of Viagra would go out of business!'

It was a typical Fleur Bonnier remark – slightly naughty, slightly self-aggrandizing, and totally exasperating for her daughter.

Long experience had taught me that responding to that kind of provocation would only make things worse, so I concentrated on my pork and apple sauce. Fleur turned her attention to her granddaughter. 'And what about the Jools Curtis sex life? Any handsome young bucks on the scene?'

I was quite interested to hear if Fleur could elicit a more detailed response on the subject than I ever could. But all we got was: 'None I'd tell you about.'

'Why?' asked Fleur coquettishly. 'Afraid of me muscling in?'

Jools had the nerve to find this funny. Or was she just doing so to annoy me?

Fleur recognized that she was not going to get any further with her granddaughter on the subject of sex, so changed direction. 'And work? How's that going along?'

'Good.'

Fleur appraised the garment Jools was wearing. A calf-length jumpsuit in shocking pink, decorated with large white spots. 'One of your free samples, is it?'

'Dahling, I only wear free samples.' Jools said the line in a fairly accurate impersonation of her grandmother.

Fleur was delighted. 'So sensible, dahling,' she responded. 'Clothes have a definite sell-by date. I think it's like that thing about guests and fish: they smell after three days. Clothes get a bit tired when you wear them more than three times.'

'More than once, I find, dahling,' said Jools, still over-dramatizing.

She works for an online fashion magazine, which is her perfect job. From very early on, Jools always loved clothes – but never loved them for long. Her threshold of sartorial boredom was very low. She always wanted something new. This was the source of the many rows we had, particularly during her teenage years. She seemed unable to take on board the fact that I couldn't afford to keep replacing her wardrobe while it was still full of wearable stuff. I also disapproved – and she knew I disapproved – of treating clothes as disposable artefacts.

So, her current job suits Jools perfectly. An endless round of catwalk shows and label launches . . . and enough freebies for her never to wear the same clothes twice.

'Well, at least you've made an effort,' said Fleur, pointedly, to Jools. My mother was elegant, as ever, in grey linen. She's one of those women who doesn't have any everyday clothes. She is always dressed up. And, I have to admit, she always looks damned good.

Her last sentence was of course another gibe at me, one of those produced so frequently that I had long ago given up dignifying them with any reaction. The (not very subtle) subtext was: At least you and I, Jools, have made an effort. Unlike your mother.

Spending my week in Pacific Blue SpaceWoman livery, all I want to do at weekends is slob around in jeans and a T-shirt. Fleur doesn't understand this – or claims not to understand it. She doesn't possess a pair of jeans and, if she had a T-shirt, it would be called a 'top', have a designer label and cost fifty times more than the kind of T-shirts I buy. I let the remark pass unchallenged.

But Fleur hasn't yet completed her cycle of aggravation. 'I always think Sunday lunch should be an occasion. A family occasion.'

This is straying on to dangerous ground. Given the list of partners with whom, over the years, my mother has shared Sunday lunches, she is in no position to extol the virtues of family occasions.

But then, for different reasons, neither am I.

'Anyway,' said Fleur, pressing in the point of another needle, 'how's the cleaning business going?'

Though entirely predictable, this is a more difficult subject for me to curb a reaction to. It's been a matter for contention since I first started SpaceWoman. Though I've described to her many times exactly what it is that I do, she still insists on describing it as 'cleaning'. She even takes pleasure in introducing me to her new friends with the throwaway line, 'This is my daughter Ellen. She's a cleaner.'

Why my mother has to snipe away at me all the time, I don't know. My knowledge of psychology suggests that it must arise from an insecurity of her own. Because of some deep-seated paranoia, she feels the need constantly to assert her superiority over me. Which is strange, because I have never been competitive with her in the areas of life about which she cares. I've no desire to act. I've no desire to be fatally attractive to men. And I've never possessed either talent.

Funny, I reckon I'm pretty good at working out the psychology of my clients. Nearer to home, it seems, I just can't hack it.

Anyway, I manage to suppress the burning instinct to snap back and tell her I have plenty of work. The question was only asked to rile me. She's not interested in the answer.

The rest of lunch is spent in Fleur asking Jools about the fashion shows she's recently attended and trying to cap each tale of glamour with some recollection from her own glittering past. I have little to contribute to the conversation.

Besides, I'm preoccupied. I can't switch off the recurrent image of what I'd seen in the sitting room of a cluttered flat on the Hargood Estate in Portsmouth.

I don't think it would ever occur to either Fleur or Jools to offer to help tidying up after Sunday lunch – or any other meal, come to that. Jools did a bit round the house as a teenager, but always with much reproachful sighing. Now she's always busy, busy, having to rush off and catch a train back to London. Can't stay too long in a place like Chichester, can't risk getting infected by the torpor of the provinces.

Fleur agrees with her whenever the subject comes up. 'Of course, I'm basically a London person,' she says. 'Wasn't it

Oscar Wilde who described the country as "a kind of healthy grave"?'

'No,' I said the first few times she came out with this. 'It was the Rev. Sydney Smith.' Now I don't bother. My mother's conversation is studded with cherished misquotations.

Nor do I bother pointing out that her current comfortable circumstances are solely attributable to the fact that her husband Kenneth's lucrative solicitor's practice is based in Chichester. 'London person' she may be, but her income derives from the provinces, and the 'London' aspect of her personality is now restricted to shopping raids on Harrods with Kenneth's gold card.

I had just got the kitchen back to my standard of cleanliness (a slightly higher level than that aspired to by either of my children) and made myself another cup of coffee. What with changing the sheets and getting lunch ready, I hadn't had time to look at the paper.

I sat in my favourite armchair in the kitchen, just where it catches the afternoon sun, and picked up *The Observer*.

Before I could open it, the phone rang.

Hilary. 'Just wanted to say – wonder of wonders – Philip is actually here. He'd love to see you, if you did care to drop over . . .'

I was divided. Half of me just wanted to stay at home with the paper, maybe indulge in a slight doze. The other half was worried, after recent traumas, about the idea of being on my own. I knew how quickly bad thoughts could fester in solitude.

That half won. 'What time would suit?' I asked.

'When you like. Philip and I had a light brunch, so we'll be eating early.'

'I'll see you in as long as it takes,' I said.

# FIVE

Philip Boredean had aged well. His black hair had grizzled to a kind of gunmetal colour, and he didn't carry much more weight than when I first met him. Though he was rarely seen in leisurewear, he carried if off with some style. The polo shirt and jeans were artistically faded and his dark blue deck shoes, worn sockless, looked as they might at some point have made contact with a deck.

He greeted me at the gate of the cottage's front garden, having just risen from a metal table where he and Hilary had been catching the last rays of the sun. There was a bottle of rosé lolling in an ice bucket. Glasses, bowls of olives, crackers, hummus and tzatziki decorated the surface in a random way that could have been posed for a colour supplement photograph.

As always, he enveloped me in a huge hug. As always, I felt nothing more than comfort in the contact. The fact that we had once been lovers had left no mark on my physical memory. It had been a long time ago – nearly thirty years, for God's sake – and, in retrospect, not that important. We had both moved on, I'm sure, to more fulfilling sexual experiences. I certainly had. I just felt pleased that things had worked out for Philip with Hilary. Both had travelled a fairly bumpy relationship road before finding each other.

She had risen more slowly from the garden table and we exchanged 'mwa mwa' kisses on each cheek, a silly habit we'd got into over the years. Although there are no complications of a romantic nature between the three of us, Hilary always behaves slightly differently when Philip is present. It's particularly notice-able in West Wittering. Nothing major; she's just more watchful, as if perhaps she's afraid he'll get bored and rush off any minute back to London and the welcoming demands of work.

I was immediately offered a drink. I said I'd have some of the rosé. Fortunately, in spite of my mother's importuning, I hadn't had anything at lunchtime. One small glass, I reckoned, wouldn't trouble the breathalyser. It was a pity. My emotional state would have been much improved by getting mildly drunk with friends, but SpaceWoman was too important for me to take the risk.

'Gather from Hil you've had a nasty experience,' said Philip.

'Yes. Bit of a downer,' I agreed.

'Very bad luck.'

'Just being in the wrong place at the wrong time.'

'Usually down here, the person who finds the body is someone walking a dog,' Philip observed.

'In London it's a jogger,' Hilary contributed.

'Yes, well, in this case, I'm afraid it was me.'

'Gather it was in the course of one of your decluttering jobs . . .?' said Philip.

I read from the semaphore of Hilary's eyebrows that her husband knew no more about the situation than that. He was unaware his wife had any connection with the Ogdens. I indicated to her that I'd taken the point on board. How much she told him about her job was between the two of them. Maybe, I wondered, they had made a pact early in their marriage that neither of them would bring work home. That might have been a mercy for Hilary. From the time we were together I remembered that, on the subject of medicine, Philip could bore for England.

I confirmed to him that I had found the corpse in the course of my work.

'And I gather from the papers that it's thought to be murder.'

'So it seems, yes.'

'Always depresses me a bit when I hear of a murder. I suppose it's because I spend my time trying to extend life, and there are people out there trying to cut it short.' He contrived not to sound pious as he said this, just frustrated. 'Had a case a couple of weeks back of a kid who'd been stabbed in the street. Some gang thing, I think, this dreadful knife culture. We couldn't save him,' he concluded ruefully.

'I haven't had a chance to look at the papers yet.' I turned to Hilary. 'Anything in them we don't already know?'

'No, just speculation.'

'Oh well, I'll catch up with *The Observer* when I get home,' I said.

Philip smiled. 'Still a bit of a leftie, are you? *Guardian* during the week, is it?'

I admitted that it was. 'Mind you, when we first met, you were full of Socialist principles too, weren't you?'

He grinned rather wolfishly. 'Maybe. Difficult to maintain those once you start making serious money, I'm afraid. When you don't possess anything, it doesn't matter, you can be as left-wing as you like. When you've got something to *conserve* . . . well, there's a clue in the word.'

I grinned too, in a way that I hoped would close the subject. I hadn't got the energy to get involved in political argument. Because I would very quickly move on to cuts in funding for mental health services and that would just make me cross.

Fortunately, that possibility was prevented by the emergence of a young man from the cottage.

'Oh, hi,' said Hilary. 'Liam, this is my friend Ellen.'

'Hi, good to meet you.' He was long and thin, dressed in a grey T-shirt and worn black jeans. Broad-chested; must've worked out in a gym somewhere. Would have been good looking but for a slight imbalance of his features. One of those over-sculpted beards which are so popular with young men.

'Liam's helping me out, kind of work experience,' Hilary explained. 'Going to do a criminology degree.'

The way he looked at her made me suspect that here was yet another of her love-struck young men. If that was the case, it didn't seem to worry Philip. Mind you, none of the previous ones had worried him. He felt secure in his ownership of a beautiful woman. The fact that other men fancied her was, for him, a kind of validation.

'Like a beer, Liam?' he asked.

'That'd be great. Thank you.'

'Criminology?' I echoed, as Philip went in to get the drink.

'Well, that's the long-term plan,' he said.

'Liam's studying law at Nottingham,' Hilary explained.

'Oh, which university?'

'Sorry?' he asked.

'My son's at Nottingham Trent.'

'Ah. I'm at the other one.'

'Wondered if you might by any chance have met.'

'What's he studying?'

'Graphic design.'

'Unlikely then. There are a lot of students round Nottingham, doing all kinds of courses.' He didn't quite make it sound patronizing.

'Of course. Well, if you ever do meet up, he's called Ben Curtis. And what's your surname?'

'Burgess. Liam Burgess.'

'I'll tell him I met you.'

'Fine.'

Philip emerged with Liam's beer. Just as he was handing it across, the mobile phone in his back pocket rang. He checked the display, said, 'I'll have to take this', and went back into the cottage.

'From the hospital,' said Hilary. 'I'll put money on it. He'll have to go back tonight. And our plans to drive up to town tomorrow morning, stopping on the way for a leisurely pub lunch . . . will go the way of many other such plans.'

Her tone was wry rather than angry. Hilary and Philip knew each other very well. And accepted each other's vagaries. Whatever romantic aspirations Liam Burgess might have had towards her, he wouldn't get any encouragement.

'So, Liam,' I asked, 'how did you come to hitch up with Hilary?'

'Like I said, I want to study criminology.'

'But you're currently studying law.'

'Yes. Nottingham only does criminology as a postgraduate degree. But I thought, if I could fit in some work experience with someone who is actually involved in that world . . . it'd stand me in good stead for the future. I sent my CV to lots of people. Hilary's the only one who responded.'

'There's always some research stuff I need doing,' she said. 'Liam's very quick and helpful.'

'Is he involved in your work at Gradewell?'

'Obviously not the one-to-one interviewing stuff.'

'I just wondered. Since he's down here.'

'Invited him down for the weekend, that's all. He's organizing the files on my laptop which, I have to confess, are in complete chaos.'

I thought, knowing Hilary's love of being in control, that was unlikely. But maybe her definition of chaos differed from mine. She always had higher standards than me. I also thought that her casually inviting Liam down for the weekend was another example of her misjudging a young man's likely responses.

Philip emerged from the cottage, loading documents into a briefcase. His wife's analysis was spot on. He had been summoned back for an emergency at the hospital. And immediately his body language expressed increased enthusiasm.

After he'd gone, the three of us continued chatting for a while, but it wasn't a very relaxed conversation. The one subject Hilary and I really wanted to talk about, the corpse I had found on the Hargood Estate, was off limits with Liam present.

And he didn't add a lot. He wasn't exactly evasive, but uncommunicative when I asked about his life. Maybe it was just his age, but I got the impression he had difficulty in concentrating on anything that wasn't Hilary.

And she chattered on, her talk uncharacteristically small, serenely unaware of his devotion.

Some half an hour after Philip had left, I too was on my way, using the excuse of a large lunch to counter Hilary's offers of more food.

Ben wasn't back when I got home. Stifling a pang of anxiety, I poured myself a large Merlot. No worries about the breathalyser now. And, finally, I settled down to read *The Observer*.

It wasn't on the main pages, which were as usual full of the idiocies of world leaders and our own politicians. Just a small report towards the back. News of a murder in Portsmouth. And, at the top of the column, a photograph of the victim's face.

It was someone I recognized.

# SIX

'Kerry Tallis,' Gervaise echoed my words when I went to see him on the Monday morning. The name of the murder victim.

'That's right. You remember her, Dodge?'

I should explain 'Dodge'. The nickname came up fairly early in our relationship. When I started SpaceWoman, I very soon realized that I was going to need someone reliable with his or her own transport to remove large amounts of clutter. Not only remove but find the appropriate place to dump or recycle the stuff. I had some unsatisfactory experiences with people who advertised themselves as 'a man with a van' – and one particularly incompetent operator who had the nerve to call himself 'a gentleman with a van'. His definition of a 'gentleman' proved to be, particularly in the close quarters of a cluttered bedroom, rather different from my own.

Finally, on the verge of giving up, I found a listing in a local freesheet, which read: 'TREASURES UPON EARTH – All of your rubbish has a value to someone.' There was a mobile number and, intrigued by the wording of the ad, I immediately rang it.

I'd been anticipating something fairly rough, but the voice which answered was even posher than that of the useless 'gentleman with a van'. Posh but slightly evasive. He identified himself as 'Gervaise' and asked how he could help.

We bonded immediately by voice on the phone, and I fixed to go and see him later that day. His instructions were very precise. To find his house, I had to turn off up a narrow farm track outside Barnham, in the direction of the nearby village of Walberton. I was to follow that as far as it went and he'd be looking out for me.

The turning would have been easy to miss if I hadn't been given such detailed instructions. The hedgerows either side of the track were overgrown, but the hard-packed earth in the parallel tyre-tracks showed regular use.

The trail ended at a broad entrance whose gate had been fixed open so long that weeds and brambles had grown up around it. There was a house, probably four-bedroomed, in dull red-brick, and a couple of outhouses with corrugated iron roofs. Everything was tidy, but unadorned.

The place had the air of a farm or smallholding, but there were no signs of cultivated crops or livestock. The space in front of the house was dominated by a pale blue drop-side truck which was clearly old but had been extremely carefully looked after. Raised outlines on the driver's side door showed where the logo of some former owner had been painted over.

(I later discovered from Dodge that the van was in fact a 1951 Morris Commercial CV9/40 Tipper. He told me that before he knew me well enough to realize how little interest the details of motorized transport held for me. But he did confirm something I'd suspected, that he'd done all of the refurbishment and main-tenance on the vehicle himself.)

That first afternoon, I didn't put my sharp-proof gloves on before getting out of the Yeti. This was, after all, an introductory call rather than one that would involve actual decluttering. I walked towards the front door of the house but, before I got there, Gervaise had emerged from one of the outbuildings.

He was a tall man, the curly brown hair and beard giving way to grey. The much-washed sweatshirt and chinos had settled into an anonymous beige. He wore battered black boots, whose scuffing showed the steel toecaps beneath.

'Hello,' he said, stretching out a large hand, but not making eye contact. He looked down at the ground. 'Welcome to my planet.'

'You must be Gervaise,' I said, shaking the proffered hand.

'And if you're not Ellen,' he said, 'the law of coincidence is being overstretched.' Another person would have acknowledged the joking element in his words, but Gervaise didn't. His eyes were still fixed on the ground. He stood awkwardly, slightly swaying for a long moment, then asked, 'Would you like a cup of something?'

Rather than gesturing towards the house, he indicated the outbuilding from which he'd just emerged. 'This is the bit I live in,' he said.

The space into which he ushered me, still without any attempt
at eye contact, was possibly the most minimalist I had ever seen.
The interior walls and ceiling were clad with planks of wood,
old floorboards liberated from skips, he later told me. And he'd
put a lot of insulation between them and the building's original
walls.

There was a single bed along one side, made up with neatly
squared-off sheets and blankets. Beside it stood a wooden office
filing cabinet and a narrow bookcase containing about thirty
jacketless hardbacks. The battered table and single chair suggested
that Gervaise didn't entertain much. And most of the wall opposite
the bed was filled by a cast-iron cooking range, much older than
either the building it was in or the adjacent house. A battered
array of non-matching saucepans littered the top. A tin kettle,
which must have been put on in anticipation of my arrival, whis-
tled insistently.

'I drink nettle tea,' said Gervaise, moving towards the range.
'All right? There's nothing else.'

I had never tried it but, keen to start our encounter on the right
note, said that would be fine. Dodge took two mismatched mugs
from the small cupboard over the stove and prepared the drinks
with practised ease.

Sorry, still haven't explained why I called him 'Dodge'. The
fact is that, in the literature of hoarding, there is a mental condition that keeps coming up called 'Diogenes syndrome'. Which
is extremely unfair to the person it's named after. Diogenes of
Sinope was an Athenian philosopher, said to have spent his life
in a large ceramic jar. He made a virtue of non-consumerist
minimalism, so there's no justice in the fact that his name has
been used to describe a condition whose sufferers do the exact
opposite. Diogenes syndrome, also known as 'senile squalor
syndrome', is applied to old people who self-neglect and hoard
compulsively.

When I first saw the Spartan minimalism in which Gervaise
lived, I made a comparison with Diogenes. It was just the kind
of idea that appealed to his quirkily educated mind, and he
encouraged me to slip into the habit of calling him 'Diogenes'.
It didn't take long for that to be shortened to 'Dodge'.

I had enormous respect for him, as one of the few genuine

men of principle I know. I've met many people over the years who talk about their principles, but very few who have actually put them into action with the dedication that Dodge has. He was brought up in well-cushioned middle-class circumstances by parents who sent him to private school. He studied economics and management at Leeds University, and started out well on the career path at an investment bank in the City of London.

I tell this like a continuous narrative, but the information that makes it up was gleaned in many years of talking to Dodge. He is reticent by nature and does not like talking about himself. He never volunteers anything of his personal history, so I've pieced it together from his hints and my own instincts.

What I do know is that something happened in his late twenties that made him completely re-evaluate his life. From minimal clues I have deduced that this might have taken the form of a mental breakdown, which might have coincided with the end of a relationship. Whatever it was, it put him out of commission – possibly hospitalized, I don't know – for the best part of a year. And he emerged from the experience a changed person.

The new Gervaise left behind the rampant consumerism of the City and moved to his current home in West Sussex. Whether he bought the house and outbuildings with money he'd saved, or with an inheritance from his parents, I don't know, and probably never will. But from things he's said on the subject of mortgages, I'm sure he hasn't got one of those. I've no idea whether he has any savings left either, but if he does, he never touches them. Knowing Dodge, I'd be surprised if he believes in having any excess money and gives any that comes in to charity. But I'm speculating there.

The lifestyle he embraced in West Sussex made him perfect for my SpaceWoman purposes. Dodge's great concern was waste. Though he doesn't ally himself to any organization like the Green Party, he is very clear in his own, slightly idiosyncratic beliefs. He was appalled by the throwaway culture of the consumerist world, and he wanted to make a personal challenge to it by his lifestyle. He spends his days out in his 1951 Morris Commercial CV9/40 Tipper, collecting the detritus of human life wherever he finds it. He then devotes enormous effort and ingenuity to seeing whether he could find some means of recycling what he's collected. Something has to be totally degraded and rotten for Dodge to find no use for it. And he feels a pang of guilt for every item that has to be consigned to the dump.

He stows his collections inside the main house. When I first went in there, I thought Dodge himself might be a candidate for hoarding therapy, but soon recognized the meticulous attention with which the piles of garbage were organized. He knew where every single item was and had plans for each one of them. The other corrugated iron-roofed outbuilding was his workshop, where he spent most of his time repairing, reshaping and finding new uses for society's rejects.

The electric and electronic equipment which people jettison with such abandon when the next update becomes available, Dodge salvages and refurbishes. Knowing they have more years of useful life, he gives them to the offices of charities.

Other items he assembles from available materials. He's very inventive, particularly with furniture. He's made tables and bookshelves from discarded and broken wooden pallets. His garden chairs are particularly distinctive, structured from pallet wood sanded to silk, their seats woven not from wickerwork but from nylon rope, blue or orange, salvaged from the south coast shoreline. No two are alike, and Dodge's craftsmanship makes them very desirable artefacts.

But he sells very few. Most of them he gives to care homes or individual pensioners to brighten up their patches of garden. He doesn't like talking about money, but over time I got the impression he only sold his works when he was really up against it.

From stray hints in what he's said to me over time, I've got the impression that he does some work for a charity, though I've never found out the details of that. If he does do it, then I'm sure he's unpaid. The breakdown – or break in his life – had left him very wary of the commercial world.

From the start, though, I established that one of the ground rules for our working relationship, if it was going to develop at all, was that I would pay him. Previous experiences with charities had taught me the dangers of basing any kind of business dealing on goodwill alone. At first, Dodge didn't like the idea, but when I made it clear that was the only basis on which I would work with him, he came round. We agreed an hourly rate (and I kept checking what other people charged for similar services to ensure that his payment level kept up).

From my point of view, our relationship works fine, and I like to think Dodge regards me as a friend. But I'm still not sure what goes on inside his head. Over the nearly eight years we've worked together, he still hasn't once looked me in the eye. And I sometimes get complaints from clients, from whose homes he has removed stuff, that he's 'surly', 'dour' or 'uncommunicative'. Other people, I know, have been put off straight away by his telephone manner and not pursued their enquiries into employing him. (When I first made contact, I must have caught him on a good day.) And even more were probably put off by the 'TREASURES UPON EARTH' listing and didn't even get as far as lifting up the phone.

Anyway, that's what Dodge is like. I have a lot of time for him. I know he is a good man, if a troubled one. And one who is wary of social contact.

I've never found out for certain what made him this way, but I've a feeling it had something to do with the relationship that ended round the time of his breakdown. I'm fairly sure it was with a woman rather than a man, but what she did to traumatize him so much, I will never know. He hasn't had any romantic attachments since, and perhaps his self-imposed monasticism is a kind of damage-limitation exercise. I have spent a lot of time with Dodge alone in enclosed spaces and there has never been any sexual element to our proximity. He doesn't appear to have any close friends, either. Except for me and, as I say, I'm never really sure of my status in his thinking.

But everyone finds their own way of coping with life, and I'm very glad that Dodge is part – even though I'm not sure what part – of mine.

And he can at times be surprisingly perceptive about the behaviour of some of my clients. I have on more than one occasion found him a useful sounding board.

Which was why he was the first person I contacted after I'd found out the identity of the corpse. He was very supportive of me when Kerry Tallis first came into my life.

It was early on in my new career. Jools remained as tough and impervious as she'd always been, and Ben was kind of settled.

They were both still at school. We were living on the money we'd made by downsizing, but it was dwindling. I needed some income, and I'd got to the point where I'd felt strong enough to move forward and set up SpaceWoman. I was very determined to make a good impression in my new role.

As with the beginnings of a lot of small businesses, I started out doing jobs for friends. One let slip in the pub her worries about an elderly relative filling up her house with old magazines. At a drinks party, another confided that her husband had filled their garage with empty oil drums. A third told me that her mother had a box in which she'd kept all her finger- and toenail clippings for over thirty years.

So, by word of mouth, the bookings increased. I didn't, at that stage, use social media. But I remember, when Bruce Tallis, Kerry's father, rang my mobile, it was one of the first SpaceWoman calls I'd had from someone I didn't know.

'Listen,' he said. His manner was perfunctory, as though he had many more important calls to make, but he needed to fix a minor detail with me first. And his voice made no attempt to hide his East End origins. 'I gather you sort out people who hoard stuff . . .?'

I confirmed that was what I did.

'Well, look, I think my wife's got a problem.'

'Oh?' I was non-committal. This was not necessarily a promising start. The last thing I wanted was to be asked to take sides in a marital dispute.

'The fact is,' he went on, 'my wife and I have been very happily married for the last eight years.' The assertiveness with which this was said also sounded warning bells. 'But recently she's started behaving in a most peculiar way.'

'In what way – peculiarly?'

'Well, look, she's always had very good dress sense, beautifully turned out. In fact, the way she dressed was one of the first things that attracted me to her. I know she'll never let me down when she accompanies me to a business function.' He hadn't yet given much indication of his wife's priorities, and it seemed to me telling that he hadn't even granted her a name.

'So, what's changed?' I asked.

'She's always bought a lot of clothes . . . and accessories, bags, shoes, whatever . . . and I've always been happy with that. It's not as if I can't afford it. She can use my gold card as much as she likes. It isn't a question of the money.' He was very insistent on that point. As if I hadn't already got the message that he had plenty of the stuff.

Again, I found the way he spoke telling. 'He' could afford it, not 'we' could afford it. Increasingly, he was referring to his wife as some kind of chattel.

'Anyway, recently her buying of clothes has got out of hand.'
'Oh?'

'Ordering lots of stuff online. You know, you can do it these days at the click of the button, through Amazon or whatever.'

I did know that. 'Yes.'

'Normally, I wouldn't have bothered about it, leave that stuff to her. If that's how she wants to spend my money, fine. But I hadn't realized the scale of what's been happening, until my daughter drew my attention to it.'

'Your daughter? She must be quite young.'

'Why do you say that?'

'If you've only been married for eight years . . .'

'Oh no. I'm talking about my daughter from my first marriage. Kerry.'

Ah, so she did get a name-check. Kerry Tallis. It was a name which was destined to stay with me. And not for good reasons.

'Nearly nineteen now. Lovely girl. She felt very unsure about telling me what'd been going on. Didn't want to look as if she was betraying her stepmother, but eventually she decided the problem was so big that it couldn't just be swept under the carpet.'

'So, what exactly did your daughter tell you?'

'We have a big house called Lorimers, up near Chiddingfold . . . don't know if you know the area?'

'Yes.' It was what my mother, when I was growing up, would have referred to as 'Stockbroker Belt'. Don't know what estate agents describe it as now. 'Hedge Fund Manager Belt', perhaps?

'Anyway, we've got a good few outbuildings, changing rooms for the pool, obviously, garages, stables, sheds where the gardeners keep their gubbins and a few others which I never go into. Last weekend, when my wife was away having a spa treatment, Kerry showed me what was inside one of them.'

He paused, willing me to prompt his revelation. Perversely, I said nothing.

'One of the outhouses – and we're talking something virtually the size of a barn here – was full to the rafters with clothes that my wife had bought online. Boxes piled sky high.' I still didn't grant him any response. 'And the strange thing about it was . . . that a lot of the boxes had never been opened.'

Now that I did find interesting. It was the first indicator I'd been given of irrational behaviour. There are plenty of spoiled women who reject clothes they've ordered when they see them at home – or when they see in the mirror that they don't look on them as they'd looked on the designers' models. And some are too rich and lazy to go through the tedious process of sending their purchases back. Rejecting the stuff without even looking at it represented another level of irrationality.

'Has your wife any history of psychiatric problems?'

'No!' He didn't like the question. 'And if I thought there was anything wrong with her mental health, I'd be consulting a psychiatrist, not a decluttering expert! This is just a problem she has, a hoarding problem, that needs to get sorted.'

'Why does it need to get sorted?'

'What kind of a question's that?'

'It's a perfectly logical question. If, as you say, the money she's spending's not important, then what is important? Are you worried by the wasteful effect her habit is having on the environment?'

'Oh, for God's sake! I don't give a shit about the environment.'

'Then why have you got in touch with me? Why, if you don't think your wife's behaviour is an expression of mental ill health, do you want me to help sort out her hoarding problem?'

'It . . . it needs doing?' he replied awkwardly – and a little evasively.

'Do you think that?'

'What do you mean?'

'From what you've said, your wife's hoarding problem is not really impinging on your life. So, I was just wondering whether it's you . . . or someone else who thinks it needs to get sorted . . .?'

'I don't know what you mean.'

'Was it your daughter Kerry who suggested you ought to do something about it?'

'Yes,' he admitted, suddenly exposed. 'Will you see what you can do?'

'All right,' I said. For one thing, he was my first client who wasn't a friend, or friend of a friend. The way he kept going on about how much money he'd got suggested my bill would get paid. Also, his narrative had got me intrigued.

'Incidentally,' I asked, 'what's your wife's name?'

'Oh?' He sounded surprised that I should bother with such details. 'Jeanette.'

# SEVEN

My first meeting with Bruce Tallis was at Lorimers, the house in Chiddingfold. The Yeti looked somewhat outclassed by the array of cars revealed in the open double garages. A Jaguar SUV, a top-of-the-range BMW, a Porsche sports car, a Mercedes hatchback.

My meeting with Bruce was again on a day when Jeanette was not there. Again, a weekend. Back then, I was so keen to get the business up and running, I didn't worry about the hours I worked. I wasn't in a position then to dictate my own terms. Jeanette was doing some detox programme in a hotel somewhere, Bruce told me.

'What toxins is she dealing with?' I asked.

Her husband didn't know. But her stepdaughter did. And, of course, Kerry was present at our meeting.

'It's just another basic spa thing,' she told me, her voice indicating that a considerable amount had been spent on sending her to the right schools. 'You know, to iron out the stress.'

Not the moment to ask what stress Jeanette Tallis was experiencing. Looking round the house and grounds in which she lived, it clearly didn't arise from money worries.

'As I said on the phone,' Bruce told me, again emphasizing the wealth, 'it's not the money I'm worried about. But Kerry was getting concerned about my wife's spending.' What was it with this avoidance of using Jeanette's name? 'Kerry really cares about her stepmother, you know.'

'It's not so much the spending,' said his daughter, 'as the hoarding aspect of what she's doing.'

I remember that first meeting with Kerry Tallis very well. Nineteen, a slender girl with long blonde hair, probably a couple of inches taller than me – say five eight. She would have been pretty, even beautiful, but for the sharpness of her nose and narrowness of her eyes; features, I'd noticed, she'd inherited from her father. It was summer and Kerry was wearing a pale yellow cotton dress with a design of grey roses on it. Her long tanned legs ended in flip-flops – not the plastic ones you buy at the seaside, but the kind where the label costs a disproportionate amount more than the raw materials. She was draped artlessly on the arm of her father's well-upholstered office chair, their closeness seeming to emphasize the control she had over him. We were meeting in his study, a room which some interior designer had based on an antiseptic vision of what a gentleman's club might look like.

Bruce Tallis himself fitted the archetype of the self-made man. I didn't know at that time, but later discovered that he'd made his fortune from printing, having invested heavily – and ahead of the game – in the new digital technology. He'd cleaned up, but still carried about him, in his palatial surroundings, the shiftiness of a barrow boy who thinks a rival is about to queer his pitch. He bulged slightly out of designer leisurewear, while his tight body language suggested he'd have felt more relaxed wearing a suit.

'Yeah, the hoarding thing, like Kerry says, that's what it's about,' her father confirmed. 'And I guess that's, like, more a woman's thing.'

Though new to the profession, I already knew that men were affected by the disorder just as much as women, but it wasn't the moment to take issue with him.

'So . . . Ellen, is it?' Maybe he just wasn't good with names.
'Yes.'

'I've got some work to get on with . . .' He gestured to his empty desk. I got the impression that most of Bruce Tallis's business was conducted face-to-face or on the phone, and that he let other people handle the paperwork. 'Then I'm playing a round of golf. I'm a member at the West Sussex,' he couldn't resist getting in. It clearly meant a lot to him. 'And I was thinking it'd make more sense if Kerry showed you where my wife's been stashing the stuff, and maybe you two take it from there . . .?'

Kerry nodded and disengaged herself from her father's chair.
'Sounds good to me,' I said.

'I just don't understand it,' said Kerry. 'I mean the secrecy. I'm not good at keeping secrets. I like to have everything out in the open.'

As we walked through the gardens – estate might be a better

word – I began to believe that, as he'd told me on the phone, Bruce Tallis never went into a lot of the outbuildings. Though everything in sight reflected a high level of maintenance – new paint on the window frames, weed-free flower beds, lawns mown to thick-pile-carpet standards – the whole place had an unused air about it. I got the feeling that its owner felt no more at ease in his home than he did in his designer leisurewear.

Kerry, though, was fully relaxed. Her upbringing had taught her that this was all hers by right.

'What stage of your life are you at?' I asked casually. 'Presumably you've finished school?'

'Oh yes, done with that.'

'Uni?'

'I started a course at Durham. Business and marketing. Gave it up after a term.'

'Oh?' I said, wondering if I was about to hear some tale of student mental health issues.

I wasn't. 'Crap course,' Kerry went on. 'Three years of that would have taught me less than half an hour's chat with Daddy.'

'Ah.'

We had reached our destination. She produced a key from her pocket to open the relevant outbuilding. It wasn't quite as 'big as a barn', as her father had described it, but it was a substantial flint-faced structure that might once have been stables.

And the moment Kerry opened the double doors, I saw the extent of Jeanette Tallis's problem. The whole of the opposite wall was piled high with boxes, many bearing the familiar Amazon smile logo (at least I assume it's a smile, though my own dealings with the company have not always given me much to smile about).

Jeanette was not only a hoarder, she was a punctiliously tidy hoarder. The boxes were piled neatly in rows, as if in a warehouse. A folding stepladder was in evidence, presumably used to lift the higher ones into position. Closer inspection revealed that, on the right-hand side wall, a new pile had been started. This only reached knee height, leaving space for many more orders to come.

Kerry Tallis cocked a cynical eye at me. 'You see the problem?'

'Yes,' I said. 'I think I must meet your stepmother.'

\*    \*    \*

My 'treatment' of Jeanette Tallis was one of the oddest experiences of my life. At the time, it gave me enormous encouragement. It made me think that I really did have an aptitude for the new career I had embarked on. Subsequent events, sadly, made me doubt that judgement.

The arrangements were made through Kerry. I suggested tentatively that I'd prefer to meet Jeanette for the first time without her husband, and there seemed to be no problem about that. 'Daddy's very rarely here except at weekends,' his daughter told me. 'He travels a lot for his work.'

Husband off at work all week, wife off having spa treatments at hotels at the weekends . . . It wasn't my place to comment on the state of someone else's marriage, but it didn't change the direction of my thoughts on the subject. Philip and Hilary also spent a lot of time apart, but they had a closeness of which I hadn't seen much evidence in Bruce Tallis's talk of his wife.

Kerry said she had better be there when we met. The ease with which the appointment was set up suggested that she didn't have too many demands on her time. Having dropped out of university, she was presumably surviving very comfortably on her father's largesse.

The date was fixed – coffee at eleven on the following Wednesday. The whole set-up was – I suppose unsurprisingly – very genteel. When I arrived, Kerry answered my ring at the front door and ushered me through to a sumptuously appointed sitting room, whose French windows opened out to a terrace of choreographed pot plants and a view of the swimming pool. Sunlight twinkled off the blue surface of the water.

The woman who rose from the sofa to greet me was very much as I had anticipated. Jeanette Tallis was so perfectly groomed that she looked as if she'd only just been taken out of the box and had the tissue paper removed. She was about the same height as Kerry, and the trimness of her figure suggested she spent time in the gym at her various spa hotels. Her blonded hair had been cut to circle her oval face, whose make-up was subtle and exact. She wore a pale blue linen shirt over wide-legged white linen trousers, and the sort of tennis shoes that cost almost as much as a tennis court.

Though I knew they were not blood relations, I noticed a

surprising similarity between her and Kerry, suggesting that maybe Bruce Tallis always went for the same type of woman. One thing was certain – as he had proudly boasted, Jeanette would never let her husband down at a business function. Nor could I imagine her feeling let down when she put on a garment she'd ordered and found the image in her mirror didn't match the one in the brochure. But that was, of course, just outward appearance. I had reason to know how different the image presented to the world could be from self-image. And what Kerry had shown me in the outbuilding dictated that Jeanette Tallis could not be as in control of her life as she appeared to be.

'Good morning,' she said, extending a hand to me. 'You must be Ellen.'

It was clear when she spoke that Bruce Tallis had not only got a perfectly packaged second wife, but that with Jeanette he had also moved a few rungs up on the social ladder. Her vowels bore witness to the fact that she had been to the same right schools as her stepdaughter.

I shook her hand and was gestured to a sofa. Kerry sat down beside me. Jeanette descended gracefully back into her armchair, very much the *grande dame*. 'Now, Ellen, would you like coffee? Tea? Something else?'

'Coffee would be very nice, thank you.'

'Coffee, please, Ramiro,' she called across the room.

'Yes, Mrs Tallis,' I heard from behind me. He must have been in the kitchen doorway, waiting for the order. A stocky man with black trousers and a white shirt under a black waistcoat. His clothes were sufficiently like a uniform for me to wonder what title he was given in the Tallis household. Given their level of pretentiousness, I wouldn't have been surprised if it was 'butler'.

By unspoken but mutual agreement, we didn't embark on the subject of our meeting until we were all equipped with cups of excellent coffee (brought in, incidentally, not by Ramiro but by a short dark woman, his wife perhaps, taking the role of housekeeper). Till then, we talked inconsequentially about the good weather, a constant source of surprise to the British, and how fortunate it had been to ensure an uninterrupted Wimbledon fortnight. I got the impression Jeanette had been watching every second of the coverage.

'Bruce is not interested in tennis,' she volunteered. 'Golf's his game. He's a member at the West Sussex, you know.' She seemed as keen as he had been to mention this fact. 'Try to keep him away from the television when one of the Majors is on.'

Finally, as the kitchen door closed behind the housekeeper, I decided we'd had enough small talk. 'You know why I'm here, Mrs Tallis?'

'Oh, please call me "Jeanette".'

'Very well, Jeanette. But you do know why I'm here?'

'I suppose so,' she responded with airy charm. 'Kerry did mention something about my clothes-buying habits.'

'Yes.'

She shrugged. 'I like clothes. I always have.' She dropped into a little girl voice. 'Is it so unusual for someone of our gender to like clothes?'

'No, it's not unusual,' I agreed. 'It's really a matter of scale.'

'Oh?'

'Buying clothes is perfectly natural – and so long as you can afford them, it's not a problem.'

'Well, honestly, darling . . .' Jeanette gestured winsomely around the huge sitting room and the view of the garden. 'I don't think you need worry about that. Bruce does look after us very well.'

'Yes, I'm sure he does.' I hesitated as to which direction to go in, something I wouldn't do now. My SpaceWoman years have greatly improved my client skills, but at that stage I was still feeling my way. 'The fact is, Jeanette, there does come a point where buying excessive amounts of clothes might be a sign of something more serious . . .'

'Oh, are you saying I'm bonkers? Due to check in at the funny farm? Like Imelda Marcos?'

'No, I am not saying that,' I replied evenly. 'But, whether she wore them all or not, Imelda Marcos did at least get her shoes out of the boxes.'

Jeanette Tallis stared at me for a second, then abruptly turned away and focused a look of reproach on her stepdaughter. 'Have you shown her the Old Stables?'

Kerry shrugged helplessly. 'I had to, Jeanette. I've been getting really worried about you.'

'It's not your business to worry about me. I'm fine.'

Kerry gave me a 'See what I mean?' look. I tried again with Jeanette. 'Can I ask you why you have so many clothes stowed away there? In the Old Stables?'

'I'd have thought the answer was obvious.'

'Not to me.'

'Well,' she said on a laugh, 'because all of my wardrobes are full!'

I did not allow this attempt at humour to deflect me. 'It still seems to me to be unusual behaviour,' I said.

She was riled now. 'It may seem that to you, but may I ask what bloody business is it of yours?'

Before I had a chance, Kerry was answering for me. 'Ellen is a declutterer. She helps people who have problems with hoarding.'

'I do not have problems with hoarding!' Jeanette spat out. 'And I wish you'd bloody get off my case!' This was addressed to her stepdaughter, not to me.

'I'm not on your case,' said Kerry, infinitely reasonable. 'I want you and Daddy to be happy. I'm just trying to help you.'

'The day I need help from you I'll be in a sad state!' Jeanette flashed back.

'Listen,' I said, trying to maintain the peace, 'if you wouldn't mind my just making a preliminary assessment of what's been happening . . .'

'And what would that involve?'

'If you wouldn't mind, I'd like you to show me your wardrobes in the house . . .'

Her well-brought-up politeness did not allow her to give a flat refusal to the suggestion. 'I can't see what possible use that could be to you.'

'And then if we could both go and have a look at the Old Stables . . .?'

'Again, I don't see how that's necessary.'

'It would help me make my assessment,' I said.

'Yes, go on, Jeanette,' Kerry urged. 'Let's do as Ellen says, and have a look at your dressing room.'

'Very well,' said her stepmother, defeated.

The wardrobes upstairs gave no sign of being owned by a hoarder. The design of the master suite provided two huge his-'n'-hers dressing rooms either side, adjoining two his-'n'-hers bathrooms behind the bedroom's back wall.

Jeanette's built-in cupboards were arranged as if ready for a military inspection. There were sections for dresses, skirts, trousers and tops, neat drawers for underwear and accessories. And I couldn't help noticing that, on stands on her dressing table, there was a lavish display of expensive jewellery. Whether Jeanette herself kept everything so regimented, or whether it was done by the housekeeper or other staff members, for many women it would have been the dream dressing room.

And, though it contained more clothes than most could afford, there were not more than would be needed by a wealthy woman who was required to attend many business functions.

I had of course already seen the contents of the Old Stables, but I was intrigued to witness how Jeanette Tallis would react to someone else being allowed into her private domain.

As before, Kerry led the way across the garden and unlocked the doors. As they were opened, I observed no change of expression on Jeanette's face.

Kerry, about to speak, was interrupted by the ringing of her mobile phone. A quick look at the screen told her it was someone she wanted to speak to in private, so she moved away from us.

The moment she did, I felt the fierce grip of Jeanette's hand on my arm. 'You know what she's trying to do, don't you?' she hissed. 'She's gaslighting me! She's trying to make me think I'm going mad!'

'Are you sure?'

'Of course I am. This is all a set-up. That's why she rang you.'

'But it wasn't Kerry who rang me.'

'No?'

'No. It was your husband. Bruce.'

The look Jeanette Tallis focused on me when I said that really did make me worry about her sanity. It was positively beatific.

# EIGHT

Quite honestly, I didn't know how to proceed. As I said, I'd only just set up the business, I was feeling my way. And, after recent events, my confidence was still very low. There was no doubt that Jeanette Tallis had a problem, but maybe it was one that needed the services of a psychiatrist rather than a novice declutterer.

I considered consulting Hilary about the case – she was training as a psychotherapist by then – but my pride wouldn't let me. Though she never came across to me as judgemental, to be consulting outsiders so soon into my new career seemed to me like a cop-out.

But what could I actually do to justify the generous daily rate that Bruce Tallis was prepared to pay for my services? I had by then come to an arrangement with Dodge, so if it got to the point of emptying the Old Stables and returning the contents to the various suppliers, I felt up to organizing that. I thought, however generous their 'free returns' policy might be, the scale of Jeanette's buying would require special measures. There'd be a lot of paperwork involved, but I was prepared to take that on.

Of course, none of this could happen without the perpetrator's agreement. Bruce Tallis just wanted the problem to go away, he wasn't up for hands-on involvement. And, though Kerry would, I'm sure, have been more than ready to act for her stepmother, that was not the point. The directive, the impetus to stop the hoarding and start emptying the Old Stables, had to come from Jeanette herself.

What surprised me – and made me feel almost guilty for having my problems so easily solved – was how quickly that directive came.

I had a call the very next day from Jeanette Tallis, sounding very composed and businesslike. Nothing in her manner suggested that our last encounter had involved discussion of her mental health.

'Ellen,' she said, 'I have decided I do want you to empty the contents of the Old Stables.'

'Well, that's a relief. Are you feeling—?'

But Jeanette Tallis was not about to discuss her feelings. 'Make the arrangements as soon as possible. If there are any details you need to talk to someone about, contact Kerry in the first instance. She'll consult me if necessary. Whatever you do, don't involve my husband. He's far too busy to get caught up in domestic details like this. Now, when would you be able to start?'

'I could come over tomorrow and begin to make an inventory of the stuff.'

'Fine. Neither my husband nor I will be here. We're going to Paris for a few days, staying at the Georges Cinq. Not a business trip, you understand. Time out for just the two of us.' This seemed to give her great satisfaction. 'Kerry may well be here tomorrow, I don't know about her movements. But I'll make sure Ramiro and Constancia know you'll be coming, so they'll recognize your rather comical little car.' I didn't have time to respond on the Yeti's behalf, as she went on, 'And the sooner you can get the job finished, the better.'

She spoke as if the problem was one that had been foisted on her, rather than of her own making.

'One thing . . .' I managed to interject. 'The companies to whom the stuff is returned will probably insist on having invoices.'

'You'll find all of them either inside the boxes or taped on the outside. And, as I said, the sooner you can sort the place out, the better.'

Again, she spoke as if the task for which I had been brought in had nothing to do with her.


I enjoy jobs that have a finite end. That's part of the appeal of decluttering to me. You start with a space that's full to overflowing with stuff, and you end up with an empty space, into which less stuff can be put in a more organized way. My fear of being overwhelmed by the size of a task has diminished with experience, but it's still always there.

From a child, I knew that everything was achievable. The lack of parenting I received from Fleur made me self-reliant. For every task, the only commodity required was time. So, I have developed the skill of reducing jobs to manageable component parts. If I clear that lot today, then I will have more space to clear *that other* lot tomorrow . . . Set yourself small, attainable goals, that's my mantra. And I've followed the same principle in managing my emotional life too. After any reverse, take small steps forward. That attitude will help you deal with the inevitable steps backward.

Oh dear, there's me sounding like some glib self-help guru. When my own life is filled with so many examples of that advice failing.

Anyway, what I'm saying here is that the technicalities of the challenge at the Tallises' Old Stables appealed to me. Unlike many of the jobs I would encounter, the environment was clean. I wouldn't be up against fungus, maggots or rodents. Also, the space was organized, even though there might be question marks over the sanity of the person who organized it.

Before I left home, I didn't move the flattened cardboard boxes from the Yeti's boot, but I did add some collapsible large plastic containers. Though the post-Wimbledon good weather showed no signs of breaking, I knew I'd have to stack some of the Old Stables boxes in the open, and I didn't want to risk rain damage, particularly as the goods were all being returned. I was still learning, adding items to my SpaceWoman kit as the need arose.

There was no sign of any of the Tallises when I arrived sharp at nine the following morning. As Jeanette had promised, the staff were expecting me. It wasn't Ramiro who answered the door, but the short, dark woman who'd brought the coffee on my previous visit and who I now knew was called Constancia. I think, from the names, they were probably Portuguese. A husband and wife couple, as I'd surmised, who ran the Tallises' estate.

She introduced herself, handed me a key to the Old Stables, and invited me to come in through the house. But I had my small trolley of equipment with me, so I said I'd go round the outside.

I also refused offers of coffee and tea. I had a bottle of water with me and preferred to be independent in a situation like this. Whether Constancia knew why I was at the house or had a view on the contents of the Old Stables and how they had got there, I had no means of knowing. And I'm sure she was far too professional to pass comment on her employers' behaviour.

Once I was at the location, I opened the Old Stables doors
and cast a more professional eye on the stack of boxes inside.
Remembering the collapsible ladder, I hadn't brought one of my
own.

I had planned my approach to the task. As I moved each box, I
would make a note on my laptop of the details from its receipt.
I would then group the garments in my plastic containers,
according to where they had come from. Though many had been
ordered through Amazon, a lot had come from individual
designers.

In the moments when I got bored with shifting boxes – and
there were quite a few of them; it wasn't the most stimulating
work I had ever encountered – I would get on the mobile and
check the returns policies of the various companies involved. As
I suspected, it was not going to be as simple as just taking the
boxes down to the Post Office. The scale on which the ordering
had taken place, and in many cases the time that had elapsed,
meant that their ordinary agreements did not apply. Some of the
firms flatly refused to take the goods back, and those who did
wanted them delivered to depots somewhere.

The task was a very boring one but, as I said, it was finite. I
could look ahead to a time when it would be completed. I was
very diligent about the paperwork; I knew I was doing an efficient
job. My competence gave me confidence. Though I hoped that
future commissions might be more interesting, I began to believe
that I could make a go of SpaceWoman as a business.

And of course, I was being paid. Bruce Tallis, unwilling to
get involved in detail, had agreed so readily to the hourly rate I
proposed that I wished I'd asked for more. But the terms were
still generous.

One thing I couldn't help noticing was that my work was being
watched. By Ramiro, the 'butler'. The first couple of times he
came out on to the paving round the swimming pool, I thought
it was on some domestic chore. But it happened too often for
that explanation to hold water. I wondered if he was checking
to see that I wasn't skiving. And if that were the reason, was it
his own curiosity he was satisfying? Or was he following orders
from a suspicious employer?

The more dealings I had with the companies from whom the

clothes had been bought, the more I realized I would need transport to return the goods to various depots around the country. This was the perfect job for Dodge, whose services I had by then used a few times. But it would incur further expenditure that I had not cleared in my initial talk with Bruce Tallis.

So, following his instructions, I rang Kerry's mobile. It seemed a long time before she answered, and when she did, her voice was bleary, as if she'd just been woken up. I had no idea where she was speaking from, one of the few drawbacks of mobile phones.

She quickly agreed to the additional expense of employing Dodge, and then asked how I was proposing to handle the refunded money.

'I was going to ask you that, Kerry. I mean, we are talking about five figures here. Presumably – what . . . it would go into your mother's bank account?'

'I'll have to check that with Daddy,' she said, as if I were making some great imposition on her time.

'Well, if you could let me know as soon as possible. Some of the companies are happy to just put the money back on the card with which the clothes were bought. Others are less accommodating.'

'OK. Leave it with me. I'll talk to Daddy today.'

'Oh, of course, he and Jeanette are in Paris, aren't they?'

'Yes, he's bribing her with luxury again.' I thought that was an odd thing to say but passed no comment. 'Don't worry,' she went on, 'Daddy'll stop anything to take a call from me.' She giggled. 'I'll call you with the bank details later.'

Which she duly did.

It wasn't as simple as just sending Dodge off with a load of boxes and addresses to deliver them to. The details were so complicated that I had to join him in his immaculate 1951 Morris Commercial CV9/40 Tipper.

Kerry was at Lorimers the first time he appeared. Dodge was at his shyest and she showed no interest in him at all. Nor in me either, come to that. The business between us was concluded, and she had no expectation of meeting me again.

To my surprise, though, there was one person on the premises who seemed to have been impressed by my performance, and

that was Constancia. As Dodge and I were sweeping out the Old
Stables after we'd put the last load on to the Tipper, she came
out of the house towards us.

'You have done a good job,' she said.

'Thank you.'

'You work hard. I have watched you through the kitchen
window.'

I couldn't help saying, 'You haven't watched me as much as
Ramiro has.'

'Ah.' She spread her hands wide. 'My husband, he always prefers
to watch other people working than doing anything himself.'

I grinned. I wasn't about to make any further comment. She
could criticize him; it wasn't my place to do so.

'He has dreams, Ramiro. He has dreams of saving enough
money to go back to Albufeira and opening a restaurant there.
He says soon we will have money, enough money. I do not believe
him. It is another dream, a fantasy. You see, though Ramiro would
do anything for money, he is not good at saving it. The restaurant
in Albufeira will remain what it always has been – just a dream.'

'I'm sorry,' I said, because it seemed appropriate.

'Don't be sorry for me,' Constancia responded with a harsh
cackle of laughter. 'If the restaurant ever opened, guess who
would be doing all the work to run it?'

I grinned the automatic grin of gender solidarity.

Constancia gestured towards the empty Old Stables. 'This is
a strange job you have to do here,' she said.

Once again, I didn't pass comment, unwilling to sound critical
of Jeanette Tallis.

'The rich, they have ways of their own,' Constancia observed.
'Well, you have done a good job,' she repeated, and went back
into the house.

The paperwork was fiddly, and there was a lot of waiting around
depots while the right person to deal with the return of goods
was found. Despite my having agreed terms on the phone with
most of them, there was still plenty of haggling to be done. Even
though none of the boxes had been opened, some of the companies
were unwilling to give full refunds on styles bought over two
years before. I certainly earned my daily rate.

But the great bonus of the expeditions was the opportunity it gave me to spend time with Dodge. Though he still never looked me in the eye, those hours spent in the Tipper forged a bond between us. By the time the last return had been made, I felt I had someone in my life who would support me in any crisis.

At one point on that drive back, I observed, 'Well, I have the satisfaction of a job well done, but I hope all of the things I take on aren't as boring as this one.'

Dodge grinned. 'The two main elements of life are boredom and terror. Of those, boredom is preferable.'

By then, knowing his love of quotations, I asked, 'Who said that?'

'I did,' Dodge replied.

That evening, when I got home, before I started cooking supper for Jools and Ben, I printed up my bill for Bruce Tallis. I had taken delivery of some quite swish-looking SpaceWoman invoice forms, and I relished making one out to my first client who wasn't a personal friend. It was proudly numbered '0001'. I wondered whether I'd ever get to '1000'.

I billed for four full days' work and included the costs of hiring transport. I would pay Dodge direct.

I looked at the completed invoice with satisfaction and emailed it off to Bruce Tallis.

Slowly paid bills – or unpaid bills – were, I had been warned, a regular feature in the life of a small business. Advice varied as to how long was the proper time to wait before chasing payment. But most authorities seemed to agree that a polite email request after a month was entirely legitimate. So, I sent one to Bruce Tallis. It elicited no response. A week later I sent another. Still nothing.

By then I needed the money. I had kept going with one or two minor bookings, but nothing on the scale of what I now thought of as the 'Old Stables job'.

I decided I couldn't wait any longer. I didn't relish what I had to do, but I knew it was part of the job and something I must inure myself to. I dialled Bruce Tallis's mobile number.

He answered straight away.

'Good morning. This is Ellen Curtis of SpaceWoman.' I kept my voice deliberately even. I was determined to avoid the excesses of anger and frailty.

'Oh, is it?' he snapped back. 'Well, I'm surprised you have the nerve to ring me.'

'I have the nerve to ring you because I sent an invoice for my services over a month ago and—'

'Listen! I suggest you get off the phone bloody quickly! I've decided it isn't worth the effort of taking you to court, but if you continue to bug me, I might change my mind!'

'Take me to court? What on earth are you—?'

'In fact, when I first realized what you'd done, I was all set to bring in the lawyers, but Kerry persuaded me not to. So, the fact that you're still walking round a free woman is down to the generosity of my daughter.'

'I'm sorry.' I was finding it increasingly difficult to keep my voice expressionless. 'I don't know what you're talking about.'

'I'm talking about the money that was refunded from the clothes purchases made by my wife.'

'That was all accounted for and paid back into the bank account whose details Kerry gave me. Your wife's account, I assume.'

'My wife makes purchases on my account.' Once again, he was boasting about the extent of his wealth. 'I give her complete freedom to use my gold card.'

'Very well then. The money was paid back into your account.'

'Except it wasn't.'

'What are you saying?'

'I am saying that the money was not paid into my account. You paid it into your account.'

'But that's ridiculous. I—'

'So, I think you've got a bloody nerve to come whingeing about your crappy invoice when you've taken me for thousands of pounds.'

No attempt to keep my voice even now. 'I have not!' I bellowed.

Bruce Tallis ended the call.

Again, Kerry took a long time to answer her mobile. Again, she sounded kind of spaced out. I told her quickly and angrily about the exchange I'd just had with her father.

'Well, aren't you going to say thank you?' she asked.

'"Thank you"? To you? What on earth for?'

'I persuaded Daddy not to take you to court.'

'There's no reason I should be in court. A quick check with my bank would show that none of the return money ever entered my account.'

'That's not what Daddy thinks.'

'Well, "Daddy" is wrong then, isn't he?'

'Daddy doesn't like being told he's wrong.'

'In this case he should be. He's accusing me of stealing thousands of pounds. That's a slander against me as a person and against my business.'

'Business? Pretty tinpot business, isn't it? Hardly the sort that's going to be able to afford decent lawyers.'

'This needn't involve lawyers. You just tell your father that I have not stolen any money from him and that all I'm asking for is the agreed payment for my services, as detailed in the invoice which I sent over a month ago.'

'Ooh, I don't think I can do that,' said Kerry, annoyingly winsome.

'Why not?' An idea 'why not' was beginning to form in my head. 'Those bank details you gave me . . .' She didn't respond. 'If they weren't for your father's account . . . and they sure as hell weren't for mine . . . whose account did the money go into?'

'I've no idea,' she said, still playful.

'Unless of course it was yours . . .?'

'Hard for you to prove that.'

To my mind that was an admission of guilt. I was furious. 'If you've taken that money and told your father that I took it—'

'Who do you think he's going to believe – you or me? Listen, I have very generously persuaded him not to pursue you through the courts . . .'

'It's not that generous. My innocence could be easily proved, as I said, by just checking my bank account. And the only reason you persuaded him not to sue me is so that he doesn't find out where the money has actually gone.'

'But if Daddy thought someone was accusing me of stealing, have you any idea of the kind of lawyers he could call on to sue you? And, if you think I'd have been stupid enough to put the return money into my own usual personal account, you under-estimate my intelligence. It'd take a long time to find out where the money actually went. Indeed, the account might never be found.'

There was no question about it now. Kerry Tallis was admitting she had stolen the return money. But she continued, with infuriating confidence, 'And while that search is going on, the charges against you would still be in place. Daddy's lawyers could keep that going for a long time. And do you have the financial resources to set up your own defence team against them?'

She knew I didn't. Though Kerry had admitted to me that she'd stolen from her father, there was nothing I could do to see justice done. I wasn't too worried about the reputational damage the situation might have caused me, because I knew she'd encourage him to keep quiet about the whole business, but it looked as if there would be no chance of my getting my invoice paid. And that was a very bad outcome for one of the first major jobs to be undertaken by SpaceWoman.

Which was why any mention of the name 'Kerry Tallis' always left a sour taste in my mouth.

# NINE

'The thing I could never understand,' I said to Dodge that day I went to see him after Kerry's death, 'was why she stole from her father. Taking all the money from Jeanette's returned clothes. From what I saw of the two of them, Bruce spoiled her rotten, gave her everything she asked for. Why would she need more money?'

'Ah,' said Dodge, 'I might be able to explain that.'

'Oh?'

'The fact is that Kerry had a serious heroin habit.'

'What? Why didn't you ever mention this before?'

'I didn't know before. You know, back when you first met her, I didn't know anything about the family.'

'But do you think she was using heroin back then?'

He shrugged. 'Would explain why she needed to steal from her father.'

'Yes, I suppose it would.' I thought back to the tall, elegant, beautifully spoken girl I'd seen at Lorimers. Not the typical image of a heroin addict. Then I thought of the emaciated, tattooed, ravaged corpse I'd found in Portsmouth. Those were the kind of changes drug use could wreak on a human body.

'How do you know she's a user, Dodge?'

He looked even shiftier than usual. 'It's not really something I should talk about,' he mumbled.

'Why not?' The thought came to me suddenly. 'Are you saying that you know her because you have the same problem?'

'*Had* the same problem, Ellen, *had* the same problem.'

Was this the explanation for the breakdown he had talked so little about? It was not the moment to probe. 'So, what do you know about Kerry's problem?'

Dodge looked even more uneasy than usual.

'What's the matter?'

'It's just . . . an issue of confidentiality.'

I was ahead of him, my mind making quick connections. 'I

think I know what you're talking about. The charity work you
do . . . it's with drug users, isn't it?'

He nodded in a way that was almost shamefaced. 'It's called
"ReProgramme". In Portsmouth,' he said.

'That's where you've come across Kerry recently?'

Again, a small nod.

'And, obviously, there's an issue of confidentiality there?' Of
course. As I had insisted on from the start in my own business
. . . I went on, 'What's said in the room where you meet stays
in the room where you meet?'

'Exactly. The users wouldn't come if they thought we were
going to blab about their problems to all and sundry.'

'I fully understand that, Dodge.'

'Good.' He seemed relieved.

'But the circumstances change if someone dies, don't they?'

'I'm not sure.'

'Kerry Tallis is dead. Almost definitely murdered. Talking
about her drug use can't do her any more harm, can it?' Again,
he looked uncertain. 'Dodge, there's going to be a murder investigation. It won't take the police long to find out about her drug
use and come to the clinic she's been attending to—'

'ReProgramme's not really a clinic. It's more a drop-in centre.
We run regular courses for users.'

'Whatever it is, the police are going to be round there pretty
damned soon, aren't they?'

'I suppose so.' He was silent for a moment. 'Do you want a
drink?'

'I've never refused your nettle tea, have I?'

It was quite a while since I'd been inside Dodge's living
quarters. The only difference I noted was that there were now
two chairs, both from his own pallet designs. Whether this was
a sign of his becoming more sociable, even having a partner, or
just in response to my earlier phone call, I didn't know. And I
knew better than to ask.

While the kettle boiled, Dodge told me about the charity he
volunteered for. It wasn't funded by the social services, but it
worked closely with them. A town like Portsmouth is bound to
have major drug problems, and it too had suffered from government funding cuts.

'I go to ReProgramme a couple of days a week,' he said, continuing with disarming honesty, 'I know how easy it is to get into a state of dependency . . . and how difficult it is to get out of it. So, I . . . well . . . do what I can.'

'And who are the clients?'

He spread his hands wide. 'You name them, they're there. Every addict has a different story. Getting into the wrong company, being in care, gang culture, picking up bad habits in prison – you name it.'

'Hardly the sort of background Kerry Tallis came from,' I said, as he crossed to infuse the nettle tea.

'Addiction is wonderfully undiscriminating, Ellen. Doesn't matter what your background is, it can still catch you. Look at me – nice middle-class boy, university education, city high-flyer. People would say that drugs ruined my life.' He was silent for a moment. 'Though I'm more of the view that they *made* my life. Getting off them did, anyway.'

Again, I didn't ask for any elaboration. He passed me my mug. I took a restorative slurp, then asked, 'And it was at the ReProgramme drop-in centre that you met Kerry again?'

'Yes, but I didn't know it was her.'

'You did only meet very briefly that time at Lorimers.'

'If I'd known her for years, I still don't think I'd have recognized her. Hair dyed black, covered with tattoos and . . . the state of her body . . .'

He didn't need to say more. I had seen her.

'Calling herself "Celeste" by then. I only found out her real name because I had to check through some paperwork about her hospital admissions.'

'How long had she been going to ReProgramme?'

'Last year, I suppose.'

'And where was she living?'

He shrugged. 'Friends' places. With other druggies. On the streets sometimes.'

'You'd think, with a father who doted on her like that, someone who was so rich . . . he wouldn't have let her get into a state like that.'

'I gather he would have supported her, but she cut off contact with him. Went underground.'

I remembered when I had first met Kerry, the blonde, beautifully groomed Daddy's girl, perched intimately on the side of his chair. 'Why would she do that? Why would she cut herself off from him?'

'I'm not absolutely certain, but I think she needed a change of identity.'

'Why, though?'

'To avoid trouble with the police.'

'Oh?'

'I pieced this together from a lot of conversation with Celeste . . . Kerry. They were pretty garbled at times, but I think I got the main outline. She made no pretence about her background, she said that she'd come from a rich family. I think she intuited that she and I might have something in common in this respect, so she kind of bonded with me. Other staff at ReProgramme were very keen on that, developing personal empathy with the clients. It offered the chance of being able to get to the root of their problems. Anyway, Celeste said that her father had always been generous, but she didn't want to push him too far. She didn't, basically, want him to know about her habit, to let him preserve the image of her as Daddy's precious little girl. She said she stole some stuff from her father, and jewellery from her stepmother, but she couldn't take too much or they'd start to get suspicious. But she had a habit that was getting increasingly expensive.'

'So, what did she do?'

'She started stealing from her father's friends.'

'Ah.'

'Friends apparently from some golf club he belongs to.'

'The West Sussex. Bruce Tallis is very proud of his membership there.'

'Well, apparently one of his golfing chums surprised Kerry in the act of stealing his wife's jewellery. And when that came to light, other members also reported thefts, and it seemed pretty likely she was responsible for those too. Kerry's father apparently offered to reimburse them for what was missing, but the one who'd caught her red-handed was of the old school. Thought she ought to be arrested and go through the courts. That's when the blonde Kerry Tallis disappeared and a black-haired Celeste started hanging round on the Portsmouth drug scene.'

'Do you know if her father was still in touch with her? Did he somehow continue to send her money?'

Dodge shrugged ignorance. 'Don't know anything about that.'

'Still, at least the fact that she was going to the ReProgramme meetings meant she was trying to deal with her problem.'

Dodge twisted his lips in disagreement. 'Maybe. She was a very irregular attender. She'd come along to the sessions and, you know, when she wasn't drugged up, she sounded very rational. Cut-glass vowels, like talking to one of the genteel matrons of Chichester. Then she'd start using again and . . . disappear for weeks, be totally incoherent when she came back.'

'What brought her along to ReProgramme in the first place? Was that just her trying to get her life sorted?'

'Maybe a bit of that. But no, first time a friend brought her. That's the way it usually happens. Someone gets on the scheme, starts to make some progress, thinks of a mate with the same problem, brings them along. In Celeste's case, it was a guy called Les.'

'A user?'

'Yes. And dealer in a minor way. Had served time for dealing more than once. Just come out of Gradewell when he first came to ReProgramme. Really seemed to have seen the error of his ways, wanted to make a new start. We had hopes for him, thought he might go through with the training as a counsellor and join the staff. That's how most of us came in; had some bad experiences, thought maybe we could help people with similar problems.'

'Your tone of voice implies that Les didn't complete the training.'

'No. It was all going well, but . . . I think it was meeting Celeste that put paid to his career as a counsellor.'

'Oh?'

'There was clearly a spark between them, right from the start, first time he brought her along. I think he really thought he could help her and, who knows, if she got clean, perhaps he saw the prospect of some kind of relationship developing.'

'Do you think that was likely?'

'Who can say? A clean Kerry Tallis would have been way out of Les's league. A using, dependent Celeste would go with anyone.'

'So, what happened?'

'She, I'm afraid, dragged him down to her level. They went off together. Haven't seen either round ReProgramme for months.'

'When you say they "went off together", do you mean as a couple?'

'If you mean, was there sex involved, I've no idea. They *used* together, certainly, sourced drugs together; maybe stole together to fund their habits.'

'So you've no means of contact?'

'I've got a mobile number for Les. Whether he still uses it, I've no idea.'

'Maybe I'll try and contact him.'

'Why?'

'I want to know what happened to Kerry.'

'Why?'

'Partly just out of curiosity, but also there's an element of self-protection.'

'Oh?'

'Listen, Dodge, I was the one who found her body . . . or *a* body, I should say. I now know it was the body of someone I knew. It won't take the police long to find that out. I think it would be better for me if I were to ring them and mention the connection rather than waiting for them to come and accuse me of keeping it secret from them.'

'I see your point,' said Dodge.


So that's what I did. When I got back to the Yeti, I found the card the detective inspector had given me. The name that I'd forgotten was John Prendergast. Detective Inspector John Prendergast. I got a voicemail message.

I identified myself and said that, now I knew the identity of the murder victim, I realized that I had met her before. I didn't think it would be long before the police got back to me.

# TEN

Meanwhile, the work of SpaceWoman had to go on. In the chaos of the weekend, I'd had a call from Dorothy Lechlade, and agreed to go back to Clovelly on the Monday afternoon to meet her and her husband. I'd stayed so long with Dodge that making the two o'clock appointment in Chichester meant missing another lunch, a hardship I was well used to.

Tobias Lechlade was exactly as I had imagined him. Probably in his sixties, crumpled brown corduroy trousers, a tattersall check shirt over which he wore a green woollen cardigan with leather elbow patches, and brown lace-up brogues. His aspiration to look like a scatty academic were let down by a couple of details. The price stickers on the bottom of the brogues showed them to be recent purchases, and the cardigan had been bought ready-elbowed. It was not an old garment whose overuse had necessitated the leather reinforcement.

His fingers, I noticed, were stained from the constant tamping down of his pipes.

Dorothy was as soberly dressed as she had been on the previous occasion. Once again, something familiar about her face nagged at me.

Tobias's manner with his wife was interesting. Though probably only ten years older than her, he was very much of the 'don't you worry your pretty little head about that' brigade. Also, and I got the feeling it was for my benefit, he was constantly touching her, taking her hand, bestowing little pats on her shoulder or bottom. The gestures seemed to be statements of ownership.

I found this act mildly repellent, but Dorothy clearly lapped it up. I might have thought what an emotionally impoverished life she had had to warm to such behaviour, but I curbed such speculation. What went on inside another marriage was not my business.

'Dotty's told me why she called you in,' said Tobias. I also registered that I would hate to be called 'Dotty'. 'Secretive little minx, eh? Going behind my back. When the cat's away . . .'

Dorothy, I'm afraid, simpered at this.

'Still, I'm not criticizing her,' he went on magnanimously. 'I know that marriage – even at our advanced age – is a matter of compromise, each partner making concessions to the other in a fair and even-handed way. So, if Dotty feels that changes are needed to my workspace, I am prepared to discuss the issue . . . so long as she agrees to take up my system of stacking the dishwasher.'

Tobias guffawed. Dorothy tittered. Clearly, the dishwasher had become a private joke between them. I disguised my inward wince.

'No, I'm a reasonable man. Obviously, I'm not going to sanction any changes that will affect my working methods . . .'

'I wouldn't expect you to, darling,' said Dorothy, the endearment sounding slightly awkward, as if she didn't yet feel at ease using it.

'. . . but anything that improves my efficiency . . . well, I'm all in favour of that.'

'You'll definitely need to get the leaking roof sorted,' I said, 'and I think there's a significant fire risk from all those papers.'

'"All those papers"?' he echoed humorously. 'How easily my life's work is dismissed.'

'I'm sure Ellen wasn't dismissing it,' said Dorothy. The slight anxiety in her voice suggested to me that Tobias had a temper on him when he was crossed in anything. There had been a joking tone in his words, but I suspected his supply of bonhomie might be finite.

'Anyway,' he said suddenly, clapping his hands together, 'let us go and see the extent of my shortcomings, and what SpaceWoman can suggest to improve my life.' There was a lot of scepticism in the way he spoke my company name. He rose from his kitchen chair. 'There's no need for you to come with us, Dotty.'

When I was alone with Tobias Lechlade in his attic glory hole, I was made very much aware of the fact that we were a man and a woman alone in a room together. It's a familiar situation to all of my gender. Nothing so overt as a grope or a fumble, just a consciousness of the sexual potential. The man is probably conscious of it first, but his consciousness of it makes the woman very quickly aware of it.

Tobias's manner was immediately different to the one he'd displayed with his wife present. There was overt flirtatiousness in his words as he said, 'So, are you going to put me over your knee and spank me for my untidiness?'

'I don't think that'll be necessary,' I said, as icily as I could.

'Very well.' He moved through to the inner sanctum of his office, and casually gestured towards the shelf of books by T.J. Lechlade. Equally casually, he said, 'I don't know if Dotty showed you these when she did the Grand Tour . . .'

'Yes, she did.'

'All my own work.'

'She told me.'

'About my specialist subject, the Wars of the Roses.'

'She mentioned that too.'

'My minor contribution to that particular field of endeavour,' he said with spurious humility. 'My legacy to historians of the future.'

I made no comment. I had, amid the turmoil of the weekend, checked his publisher out online. It was one of those who offer to 'help you fulfil the dream of publishing your own book'. In other words, money would change hands between author and publishers, and the books would be print-on-demand.

Which meant that the works of T.J. Lechlade were unlikely to have been read by any other historians, and would certainly not appear in university libraries. His history writing, his whole career, was a vanity project.

Which, of course, raised the question of how he funded his very comfortable lifestyle. I got the impression that, as well as Clovelly, Tobias Lechlade's parents had left him quite a substantial private income.

But I wasn't there to speculate about his financial situation. I looked around the chaos of his study. 'The question really is, how much you do.'

'How much . . .?'

'Decluttering. By how much could these piles of papers be reduced?'

'These "piles of papers", as you describe them, do represent a lifetime of study. I would have to go through them in great detail to find which ones are no longer pertinent to my work. You see, it may look like chaos to you, but I know absolutely to the last detail where everything is, Ellen.'

As he spoke my name, he stood far closer to me than was necessary. I moved away towards the corner where the rain had come in. 'Shifting this lot would be my first priority. I'm sure any roofer you get is going to need to inspect the inside to see where the leak is. They'll need access.'

'Yes, I'm sure they will,' said Tobias Lechlade airily. 'I don't get involved in practical things like that. I let Dotty sort them out.' Presumably, when she'd been alive, he'd delegated 'practical things like that' to his mother. I was trying to restrain the annoyance that was building within me. Tobias Lechlade seemed to have led such a cushioned life. In his own tiny universe, he was the planet around which everything else orbited. I didn't envy Dorothy the marriage she was now stuck in.

Tobias's next words didn't endear him to me any further. 'I'm a free spirit, actually. Would you believe that the recent one, to Dotty, is my first marriage?'

'Yes,' I replied with some edge, 'I don't have any difficulty believing that.'

'Not that there haven't been other people who wanted to marry me in the past . . .' The only comments I might have made would have been offensive, so I said nothing. 'But, in the words of the old saying,' he continued, 'why buy a book when there's a thriving lending library in the town?'

'I don't think I can help you much,' I said abruptly. 'You need to discuss with Dorothy what you actually want to do with this space. If the conclusion you reach, between the two of you, is that you need the services of a declutterer, get back in touch with me.'

I moved towards the door. Tobias held out his arm in such a way that I could not get past him without physical contact. He grinned a grin that has infuriated women since records began, a look of atavistic gender superiority.

And then he had the nerve to say, 'Oh, come on, Ellen. I know you find me attractive, and I know you're wearing a wedding ring and all that . . . I don't wear one, incidentally. It might curb my activities a bit.'

He lowered his arm in such a way that his hand brushed against my breasts. It could have looked accidental, but it wasn't. I hated the idea of those tobacco-stained fingers being anywhere near me.

Raising his arm again to block my exit, he went on, 'Maybe we could meet up for lunch on a Friday in London . . .?'

He was spared the fusillade of responses that was building up in me, simply by the fact that my mobile rang. I looked down at the screen. Detective Inspector John Prendergast.

'I'll have to go and take this,' I said.

'Suppose I don't let you go . . .?' asked Tobias, delusionally secure in his own magnetism. Why a man with flaking skin, yellowed teeth and hair cultures in unlikely places round his nose and ears should think himself attractive was way beyond me.

'It's the police,' I said.

Amazing how quickly his arm dropped then. Probably he had no reason to fear the police, it was just an instinctive reaction.

By the time I got to the front door, I had decided that was to be my last visit to Clovelly. I felt desperately sorry for Dorothy Lechlade, but what needed doing in their marriage was way outside my job description. I hoped the scales would quickly fall off her eyes and within six months she would be securely divorced.

Once in the Yeti, I was about to call back Detective Inspector John Prendergast, when the mobile in my hand rang. I answered it.

'It's me. How're you doing, Ellen?'

I knew the voice immediately. He'd always said, 'It's me' on the phone and I'd never really worked out whether that was endearing or a sign of arrogance, assuming that everyone he spoke to knew who he was. His voice no longer gave me the frisson it did in my teenage years, but it was good to hear him. My first boyfriend, husband of my best friend.

'Philip. How're things with you?'

'I asked first,' he said.

'All fine here.' It was instinctive, and a much better response than embarking on the details of the things in my life that weren't fine (like having recently found a murder victim and – worse at that moment – having been come on to by a self-deluding academic in his sixties).

'Good to see you yesterday,' I went on.

'Yes.' There was a silence before he said, as I knew he would, 'It's about Hilary.'

'She seemed in good form. Looking as gorgeous as ever.'

'Yes.'

'Sorted out your medical emergency, have you?'

'Which medical emergency?'

'The one for which you had to rush back to London yesterday.'

'Oh, sure, that's all right. Though something else has come up now.'

'Same old Philip.'

'What do you mean by that?'

'Only that you've always had workaholic tendencies.'

'I'm not attempting to deny it. But at least it's *good* work.' There was a winsome appeal in his voice that I recognized from long ago.

'I've never questioned that, Philip.'

'No.' The conversation became becalmed.

'So?' I prompted. 'About Hilary . . .?'

'Yes. You know about this research she's been doing with lifers from Gradewell?'

'I know in outline what she's up to, yes. She obviously doesn't talk to me about individual cases.' Which wasn't strictly true, as of recently. But true enough.

'She hasn't talked to me about it in detail. But, about that body you found in the flat in Portsmouth . . .'

'Mm.'

'Lots of speculation in the press.'

'I'm sure there is.'

I hadn't actually looked at the paper that morning. But when I thought about the situation, I wasn't surprised that there had been press conjecture about Kerry Tallis's death. Journalists couldn't actually write that Nate Ogden was the prime suspect in the crime, but they could legally state that the body had been found in his mother's house and publish photographs of him. Mention that he had been serving a sentence for killing another young woman. And leave the scandal-ravenous British public to make their own conclusions.

That certainly appeared to be what Philip was doing. 'It seems,' he went on, 'that the main suspect was one of the lifers Hilary had been working with.'

'Yes. Early days in the investigation, but I can see how people might think that. What the police are thinking, where they've got to on the case, of course I have no idea.' I didn't mention that I was about to speak to the chief investigating officer.

'I'm just worried, Ellen, about what Hilary may be getting herself into here.'

'She's not getting herself into anything different from when she started the project. She knew then that she was dealing with murderers. That was the whole point of the research.'

'Yes, and I know how pleased she was to have got the funding for it. Hilary's always been amazingly ambitious, I don't need to tell you.' I wondered if perhaps he did need to tell me. I'd always put her driven nature to having high standards rather than ambition. Perhaps, in her case, the two were the same thing.

'When she started it,' Philip went on, 'she told me the project was going to be all-consuming and I said that was fine. You called me a workaholic, but I'm not in Hilary's league. We respect that in each other. It's the basis of our marriage, if you like. We both have careers that totally absorb us, but we always make time for just the two of us. But her murderers project . . .'

'Are you suggesting that that's taking her away from you?'

'No, no, there's nothing wrong with the marriage.' I felt relief. Given my position as confidante for both of them, marital problems there could put me in an uncomfortable situation. 'What I'm saying, Ellen, is that I didn't realize the level of danger in what Hilary was going to do.'

'She's very well protected when she goes into Gradewell. She's been going in and out of there for the past two years.'

'I know. Also, the lifers she was dealing with, she assured me, were people who'd committed their crimes a long time ago. From the few things she did let slip about them, they sounded a pretty harmless bunch. But now one of them's got out and immediately killed again.'

'We don't know that.'

'Seems pretty likely.'

'I'm sure, when the police make an arrest,' I said, uncharacteristically formal, 'they will make an announcement.'

'Perhaps. But from things Hilary's said to me recently, she was clearly doing a lot of concentrated work with Nate Ogden.'

'I didn't know that,' I sort of lied.

'Because he was about to be released. The focus of her thesis was on prisoners at that particular, unique moment in their lives.'

'Ah. She didn't tell me that,' I continued sort of lying. 'We're both very good about confidentiality in our work.'

'Well, I'm worried about her.'

'Don't be, Philip. Just give Hilary a call and I'm sure she'll be able to put your mind at rest.'

'I've tried phoning her, Ellen. She's not picking up.'

'Probably in one of her discussion groups.'

'I've been trying since six thirty this morning.'

'Oh.'

'Ellen, I don't know where she is.'

Philip sounded childlike in his helplessness.

# ELEVEN

I tried Hilary's mobile. It was no more responsive to me than it had been to her husband. No voicemail message, either. It could have run out of charge. She might be anywhere.

I sat in the Yeti and made a few more calls before I got back to Detective Inspector John Prendergast. I had a feeling I could be in for a long session with him. Other things needed to be sorted before I plunged into it.

I didn't know whether Les, the ex-con Dodge had mentioned, had been at Gradewell during Hilary's research there. But he might know others who'd had contact with her. Also, I wanted to talk to him about Kerry/Celeste. His phone rang but was no more communicative than Hilary's. His, however, did have an answering message, so I left my number, mentioning the Dodge connection and asking him to call me. I wasn't very optimistic of getting a result.

I phoned Queenie – I'd been hoping to pop in later in the day to see her – to say it didn't look likely to happen. Her deflation at the news, as ever, made me feel guilty.

I'd also been intending to visit Ashleigh, so I called her too. She didn't sound too bothered by the prospects of a no-show. She said Zak was fine, though I could hear him screaming above the music which, once again, was being played too loud. Still, nothing I could do about it at that moment.

Then I rang Ben's mobile. He'd still been in his bedroom when I'd left first thing, and I'd curbed my instinct to open the door and check he was all right. On the phone I told him I was about to go to the police and didn't know how long I'd be.

'Oh dear, what have you been up to, Ma? What crimes have you been keeping from me?'

'It's about the body I found on Friday.'

'Yes, of course, it would be. There's been reams of stuff about that on social media.'

Entirely predictable that there should be. I'd avoided looking

at any of it, only checking out work stuff on my SpaceWoman
Facebook page.

'Look, Ben, I don't know how long I'll be, but there's plenty
in the freezer and I'm sure you'll be able to entertain
yourself.'

'Yes.'

He sounded unnaturally perky, even a bit brittle, but I hadn't
got time to worry about that. 'You will be all right, won't you?'

'Yes, Ma.' The response was glib and automatic, and I had to
be satisfied with it. 'Might go out on the bike. Or a walk on the
Downs.'

'Fine. Weather looks a bit iffy.'

'Into each life some rain must fall.'

'Yes.'

'Oh, and, Ma . . .'

'Yes.'

'If it turns out you need someone to stand bail for you . . .
I'm quite prepared to increase the borrowing on my student loan.'

I do love my son.

The detective inspector said it would be easier if I were to come
to him. 'No police cars outside your door for the nosy neighbours,
eh? If you don't mind . . .?'

I said I didn't mind.

'Since the Major Crime Units of Sussex and Surrey merged,
we work out of offices all over the area.' He gave me an address
in the centre of Chichester. Reasoning that leaving my distinctive
SpaceWoman Yeti too near a police station might prompt the
same kind of reaction as a Panda outside my house, I parked in
a public car park a little way away.

I needn't have worried. The address I'd been given was in a
featureless office block the grottier end of South Street, near the
train and bus stations. Its business looked more likely to be
settling insurance claims than interrogating murder suspects.

Before I entered the building, I switched off my mobile, as if
I was going into a theatre. Though I wasn't certain what kind of
performance I was about to be part of.

When the inspector reintroduced himself, it was like I had never
seen him before. I must have been really traumatized on the Friday

evening. Normally I'm pretty observant, but neither the names nor the looks of the police I met then had stayed with me.

Now I did take notice of him, I found Detective Inspector John Prendergast to be a tall man round the fifty mark. His grizzled grey hair was thinning, and the cheeks of his long face were concave. He wore an anonymous dark grey suit, and his voice had a residual East London twang.

Though I hadn't really taken in the policewoman who'd been with him on the Friday, I could recognize that his colleague today was not the same one. Different gender, for a start. Introduced to me as Detective Sergeant Prasad. Of Indian origin, obviously. Small, neat, shirtsleeves and jeans, hair only a few millimetres up from being shaved bald. His voice was pure Croydon.

The office in which I was interviewed was as anonymous as the block that contained it. A desk, one chair behind, two in front. Nothing on the walls. I was offered coffee but refused. I was actually afraid that my hand would shake if I tried to pick up a cup. When I thought about it, I realized I had reason to be nervous.

Pleasantries out of the way, the inspector moved straight on to the purpose of our meeting. 'You said on the phone that, since Friday, you have realized that you did actually know the murder victim . . .?'

His tone was not accusatory, but still made me aware of how suspicious my delayed recollection sounded.

'Yes. I didn't recognize her on Friday because her hair was dyed, her face was bruised and she had . . . changed considerably since I last saw her.'

'Maybe you could fill us in on when you did last see her, Mrs Curtis?'

'Please, call me Ellen.'

He hesitated, but after minimal eye contact with Prasad, said, 'Very well, Ellen.' Was he perhaps a policeman of the old school, uncomfortable with the new informalities of his working environment? 'So, when did you last see Kerry Tallis?'

I gave him an edited version of my previous contact with the family. I did not reveal the scale of Jeanette's hoarding problem. Nor the uncomfortable conclusion of our transactions.

But Prendergast was on to it pretty quickly. If I'd thought, I'd have realized that he must have already spoken to the Tallises. 'And, so far as you were concerned, was your business relationship with the family satisfactory . . . Ellen?' He used my name as if he was checking out something unfamiliar.

'No, it wasn't,' I said, waiting to see how much he knew before volunteering anything more.

'Both sides agree on that,' said the inspector. 'In fact, Mr Tallis used some fairly choice language to describe your behaviour.'

'I'm sure he did.'

'There's no reason why I shouldn't tell you this: he said that the threat of his daughter going to the police with details of your appropriation of the return money might have given you a motive to kill Kerry.'

'Did he? And what do you think about that, Inspector?' Somehow, though I was happy to be called 'Ellen', calling him 'John' didn't seem right.

'What I think is usually dictated by the information I have. In this instance, I have an accusation against you by Mr Tallis in relation to your stealing money from him . . . and I have yet to hear your side of the story.'

'My side of the story will not take long. You presumably know the background of where the money came from?' Both men nodded. 'I agreed with Kerry that I would sort out the return of the goods and the considerable paperwork involved, and she would deal with the money paid for the returns. I assumed she meant by that that she would pay it into one of her father's accounts. From what he said to me at the time – and what he said to you more recently – that didn't happen. Kerry told him that I had paid it into my own account . . . whereas, presumably, she'd paid it into hers. All of this can be checked by looking at the statements for the relevant bank accounts, to which I assume you can easily get access. I certainly can show you mine. Because I run my own business and need to cover myself in the event of inspection from the tax authorities, I have kept all of the paperwork since I started SpaceWoman.'

'Thank you,' said the inspector.

'Though we will have to check through the statements,' said the sergeant, 'to corroborate what you're telling us.'

I spread my hands wide. 'Be my guest.'

'Thank you,' said Prasad.

'Have you any idea, Ellen,' asked the inspector, 'given the evident generosity of Mr Tallis towards his daughter, why she would want to steal from him?'

'I can only think that her heroin habit had already started, and she didn't want him to know about it.'

'How do *you* know about it?' asked Prasad, as if he'd caught me out in some lie.

'Because I read the papers and check social media,' I replied, at least half truthfully. 'There's been plenty of righteous tub-thumping there, following Kerry's death. How heroin is now the curse of the middle classes.'

Prasad seemed about to ask another question, but Prendergast stopped him with a little shake of the head. 'Ellen . . .' the inspector said, 'I know we talked about this in considerable detail on Friday, but could we just go back to why you went to Maureen Ogden's house . . .?'

'Very well.' I could have said something like: 'in *very* considerable detail', but I didn't. I was determined to curb my naturally combative instincts and be as cooperative as possible. Though I'd very little to feel guilty about, I still had no wish to get on the wrong side of the police.

So, I very patiently did a rerun of the Q & A we'd been through on the Friday. There was now a slight change of emphasis in the detective inspector's questions. He seemed more interested in Hilary than he had been then. I told him how we'd met, how we'd stayed friends, and gave him an outline of her research project at Gradewell. He responded to some of this as if it was new information to him.

'So, through this "research project", your friend actually knew Maureen Ogden's son?'

'Yes, he was – is – an important part of her study. But surely you know this.'

'I beg your pardon?'

'You rang Hilary over the weekend, asking if she knew where Nate Ogden had gone.'

He shook his head. 'It wasn't me.' He looked peevishly across at Prasad.

'It wasn't me either, Inspector.'

Prendergast grimaced with annoyance. 'The lack of liaison inside this investigation is . . .' He stopped himself, unwilling to talk about police shortcomings with me present.

'Have you met Nate Ogden?' he asked.

'No. There's no reason why I should have done.'

'Of course not. Or did you meet his mother?'

'No.'

'No.' He was silent for a moment, pulling his fingers down his long face.

'Have you tried to contact Hilary since the weekend?' I asked.

Prasad replied, 'Yes. Getting no response from her mobile. Tried her home this morning, spoke to her husband. He hasn't been able to get through to her either.'

A chill of fear ran through me. Just how far would Hilary go in pursuit of her research project? Might she have some means of contacting Nate Ogden? Might she know where he had disappeared to?

'Have *you* been in touch with her recently?' asked Prendergast.

'Saw her on Sunday.'

'Did you talk to her about Kerry Tallis?'

'Not about Kerry Tallis, no. About the murder victim, about the body I found. At that stage neither of us knew it was Kerry Tallis. And, in fact, Hilary had no reason to know who Kerry Tallis was.'

'Of course not.' A silence. 'And you'd had no contact with Kerry Tallis since the time when you dealt with her over her stepmother's hoarding problem?'

'Since the time she accused me of theft,' I emphasized. 'No, I haven't had contact with her since then.'

I hoped they weren't about to ask me whether I'd had any news of her since that time. If they didn't raise the matter of her disappearance into the Celeste persona, I wasn't about to. Basically, I had no desire to get Dodge involved. I somehow didn't think he'd react well to being questioned by the police. Within his complex personality, I had detected a streak of paranoia. And I didn't want him to have to talk about his past drug use.

They asked me a few more questions, but it was going over old ground. Eventually, an exchange of looks between the two detectives confirmed that they had no reason to detain me any longer. They thanked me politely and urged me to be in touch if I found out anything which might have bearing on the case of Kerry Tallis's murder. But I did not leave the building feeling that all their suspicions of me had been quashed.

I was surprised how tense my back was. When I got into the Yeti, my spine seemed rigid against the seatback. I did some of the breathing exercises I'd been taught to calm myself down. I looked at my watch. I'd only been in there an hour and a quarter. It felt like a lot longer.

When I'd regained some kind of normality, I wondered what I should do next. I had time to visit Queenie or Ashleigh, but the temptation just to go home was very strong.

I switched on my phone. There was a message on the voicemail.

It was from Les, the man with whom Kerry/Celeste had defaulted from ReProgramme. He wanted to talk.

# TWELVE

'Have the police been in touch with you?' I asked.

'No. Not recently.' Les sounded bewildered by the question. His voice had a rasp in it, as if he was recovering from a bad cough. 'Why should they be?'

'Think about it. They'll soon find out that you met Celeste at ReProgramme. Once they get in touch with the drop-in centre, they'll be told about you and her going off together.'

'We didn't exactly "go off together",' he complained.

'All right. But they're going to find out that you knew her. It's only a matter of time before they contact you.'

'They may not be able to find me,' he said defiantly.

'I didn't have too much difficulty.'

'You haven't found me.'

'I'm talking to you.'

'Yes,' he conceded. 'But you don't know where I am.'

'Anyway, you know we are now talking about a case of murder?'

'I still haven't got over hearing that,' said Les, sounding genuinely shocked. 'If I'd heard Celeste had died from an overdose, I'd have been sad, but I wouldn't have been surprised. She'd been heading that way for a long time. But why anyone would want to kill the kid . . .'

'You presumably don't have any idea who might have wanted to do it?'

'None. There're whole areas of her life I didn't know anything about. She came from a wealthy family, I think, but she never talked about that stuff.'

I was faced with a moral dilemma. Moments before, only a couple of hundred yards from where I now was, I'd been asked by two policemen to tell them anything I found out that might have relevance to their investigation into a murder. I was now talking to someone who had known the victim very well. And the police had yet to make contact with him. My obvious social responsibility was to give Detective Inspector John Prendergast Les's contact details.

I didn't consider that option for very long. My natural curiosity was too strong. I wanted a private session with the witness before I put the police in touch with him. And I wasn't even certain that I ever would put them in touch. Surely it wouldn't take them long to make the connection under their own steam? I had no wish to obstruct their enquiries, but I was starting to regard the investigation as personal.

I fixed to meet up with Les that afternoon.

He was where he'd said he would be, on a park bench, not far from the much-advertised Portsmouth Historic Dockyard. There were good children's play facilities within sight, but I reckoned the place would be considerably less family-friendly after dark. Still, it was a warm day. As I approached him, Les was blinking into the sun. The pallor of his face and arms suggested they hadn't seen much of it recently.

He looked wary as I approached. He wasn't about to say anything until I identified myself. 'I'm Ellen.'

He stretched out a hand to me. 'Les.'

For an addict – or perhaps recovering addict – he looked in pretty good shape. Though he was slender, the biceps bulging against his T-shirt sleeves suggested time spent in the gym. The tattoos on his arms didn't look as if they'd been done by a professional. He wore jeans and anonymous trainers. His thinning hair was cut short.

I was dying for a coffee and there was a snack kiosk nearby. But I didn't want to break the moment. I sat on the bench beside him.

'You were right, incidentally,' said Les. His voice still sounded as though he needed to clear his throat.

'About what?'

'The Boys in Blue. Had a call from them just after I'd finished talking to you.'

'Was it Detective Inspector Prendergast or Detective Sergeant Prasad?'

He shook his head. 'Somebody called Williams.'

'Ah. So, are they coming to pick you up?'

'No, Ellen . . . mind if I call you Ellen?'

'Please.'

'"Pick me up" sounds like they're accusing me of something. They only want to talk to me for background information about Celeste.'

'Of course. So, do they want you to go to Chichester?'

'No, no, they gave me an address right here in Portsmouth.' He looked at his watch. 'Said I'd be there in half an hour. I'd probably be on my way by now if you hadn't turned up.'

'What made you think I might not turn up?'

He shrugged. 'I don't know you, do I? I get a call from you out of the blue. You could be anyone.'

'I did say on my message that I know Dodge.'

'Yes,' he conceded. 'Good bloke, Dodge.' He looked rueful. 'Like a role model for me. I really admire the stuff he does at ReProgramme. I thought I could go down the same route . . . you know, get qualifications, be a counsellor, help people who're into this kind of shit. But that got screwed up after I met Celeste and – as you put it – "went off" with her.'

'Don't you think you can get back into the ReProgramme set-up?'

'I don't know. I let them down – I let Dodge down, in particular. And, of course, I let myself down – when I started using again.'

'Are you using now?'

'I haven't done anything since I heard about Celeste.'

'Well, that's a start.'

He looked at me cynically. 'Yeah? I heard on Saturday that she'd died. And where are we now – Monday? Clean for more than two days – let's string up the bunting, shall we?'

'All I'm saying is that, if the other staff at ReProgramme are anything like Dodge, I'm sure they'll give you another chance.'

'Maybe. We'll see.' His voice had a tinge of cynicism, but he was attracted by the idea.

'Incidentally, Les, I meant to say, you know, given the fact that you were . . . close to her . . . I'm sorry for your sake about what happened to Celeste.' I'd keep calling her that until he volunteered that he knew her real identity.

'Thanks. Kind of thing that keeps happening, when you're using. Sort of people you mix with. Number I've known who . . . you

know, overdose, accidentally while under the influence . . . You
get used to losing people.'

'When did you last see her?'

He screwed up his eyes with the effort of recollection. 'I don't
know. Week back, couple maybe. She lost interest in me.'

'What do you mean by that?'

'I mean I don't fool myself that I was attractive to Celeste as
anything other than a source of drugs. My dealer got killed in a
knife fight a couple of weeks back. Soon as I'd lost my supplier,
Celeste was off to find someone new.'

'New boyfriend or new dealer?'

He shrugged. 'Both possibly.'

'You don't know who she found?'

A shake of the head. 'No idea.'

'Have you seen her with him?'

'No,' he said firmly.

I knew he was lying, but I also knew I would get nothing more
out of him on the subject. Time to move the discussion on.
'Dodge told me that you know Nate Ogden.'

'Yes. Spend more than a year banged up in the same nick,
you get to know people.'

'You don't know where he is now?'

'Why should I?' The defensive response was instinctive.

'Because nobody else seems to.'

'That's not much of an answer,' he said, but he seemed to be
assessing my words, deciding what response to give. His manner
suggested he might know something.

'Has Nate got some hideout that you know about?'

He grinned. 'Good on direct questions, aren't you?'

'Well, has he?'

'If he did have – and I'm not saying he has – I'm afraid I
wouldn't tell you about it. Friend of Dodge's you may be, but
I'm not going to grass up a mate to anyone.'

'Honour among thieves?' I suggested.

The idea amused him. 'You could say that. Thieves,
murderers, drug dealers . . . pretty much comes to the same
thing, doesn't it?'

'What about the police?'

'*What* about the police?'

'Are you going to tell them where Nate might be hiding?'

'You are joking, I take it. I'll tell you exactly what I'll do when I'm with the police. I will do nothing to antagonize them. I do have some experience of this stuff, you know.' He grinned again and looked at his watch. 'I will turn up at the time we have agreed. I will be unfailingly polite. I will answer all their questions to the best of my ability. Sadly, my ability does not stretch as far as knowing such details as where Nate Ogden might lie low.'

'Right. I see. You know, incidentally, what some people are assuming about him?'

'I don't know, but I can guess.'

'That, because Celeste was found in his mother's house, and because Nate was in prison for having killed another young woman, and because he's disappeared since the murder . . .'

'Yes. I can join the dots.'

'And what kind of picture do they make when they're all joined up?'

'I'm not into pictures much,' he grunted.

'Do you think there's a possibility that Nate killed Celeste?'

'You can call her "Kerry" if you like. I do know who she really was.'

'Right. And do you know of any connection between her and Nate Ogden?'

'No direct connection, no.'

'Which suggests you might know an indirect connection . . .?'

'I don't think you'll think it's important.'

'Try me.'

'Well, one thing you do get a lot of in the nick is time. And time means you talk a lot . . . and if there's someone you get on with . . .'

'Like you did with Nate?' I prompted.

'Yeah, we talked a lot inside Gradewell. It's fairly relaxed there. We worked on the vegetable garden together, Nate and me. Wouldn't probably have been bosom buddies in any other kind of situation, but inside . . . well, you don't have that much choice. So, we talked a lot.'

'Did he talk about his crime? You know, the reason he was banged up. Did he mention that girlfriend, you know, the one he—'

'No, you don't really do that in the nick. Well, some do, the loudmouths. Boasting about what they done, bigging up the violence, so's they come across as real hard men. But Nate wasn't like that. Quiet type, really. He did once mention that the girlfriend had had a son who'd been taken into care before he met her. Otherwise, her name never came up. Nate did talk about his mum, though.'

'Were they close, do you reckon?'

Les sucked his lower lip. 'I don't know. The way he talked about her, she was definitely a few sandwiches short of a picnic. Filled the house full of shit she didn't need. I think she'd always been heading that way, but apparently it got worse when Nate was banged up for murder.'

I made a mental note of that. A lot of hoarding behaviour seems to be triggered by some personal trauma. But I didn't tell Les that I knew about Maureen Ogden's problem from having witnessed the results of it.

'Apparently, one thing Nate's mum was very into was coupons.' I made no response to that either. 'You know, those things you get in free newspapers, on cereal packets, all over the bloody shop.'

'I know.'

'She couldn't resist them. Forever snipping them out, forever claiming things like free pizzas and samples of washing powder and discounts on every bloody thing under the sun. Mostly useless tat, according to Nate. But she also liked these prize draw things, you know, "your chance to win a hundred grand", all that stuff. She'd been entering those for years. And, according to Nate – he told me this just before I was released from Gradewell – one day she got lucky.'

'His mum's number came up?'

'Exactly. And, incidentally, Ellen, this is another piece of information that I will not be sharing with our jolly Boys in Blue. If asked about Nate's mum, I will not divulge everything he said about her. I'll say he mentioned her hoarding tendencies, but I will not mention her love of coupons. Nor the fact that she got lucky with one of them.'

'You mean . . .?'

'Yes, she had a winner.'

'Do you know how much?'

Les shook his head. 'Nate was a bit coy about that. Certainly in the thousands, though.'

'So, from being a poor little pensioner, Maureen Ogden suddenly became a rather better-heeled little pensioner?'

'Yes.'

'With a very healthy bank balance.'

'You would have thought that, wouldn't you? Except Maureen Ogden was one of the old brigade. Didn't believe in banks, according to Nate. Kept any money she had in a shoebox underneath her bed.'

'Ah.' I suspected that I knew the answer, but I still asked, 'And why is this significant?'

'It's significant because I told Celeste about Nate's mother's win.'

That put a new complexion on things. The scenario was dependent on a high degree of coincidence, but it was possible.

Kerry Tallis, or Celeste, as ever in need of money, remembers Les telling her about Maureen Ogden's win on a prize draw. And about her distrust of banks, her habit of keeping her money under the bed. Celeste goes to relieve the old woman of the cash, and is surprised in the act by Nate Ogden, who has just witnessed his mother's death in Queen Alexandra Hospital. In his fury at what the girl is doing, Nate kills her. Realizing how he's screwed things up, he does a runner.

Hmm . . . I wasn't entirely convinced. Some of the details were a bit inconsistent and hazy.

But it was a possibility worth considering.

I had felt the vibration of an arriving text on my phone while I was talking to Les but, not wanting to interrupt our conversation, didn't look at it until back in the Yeti. I was very relieved to see that it came from Hilary.

It read: 'I've located Nate Ogden. He's at this address.' She gave me a postcode. 'I'm going to see him. I think he'll talk to me. Should be there about five. If you're interested, come along. Love, Hilary.'

Interested? I tried ringing to get more information, but there was no response. I loaded the postcode into the Yeti's satnav and set off.

As I drove back east, the synapses in my brain were popping like sparklers. The fact that I had only been given a postcode must mean that Nate's hideout was not in an urban street, but somewhere off the beaten track. And why did I have this feeling that the postcode was somehow familiar? The satnav was taking me inland, to the north of Chichester.

I felt relieved that Hilary was all right. I didn't think about ringing Philip to set his mind at rest. If she was contacting me, surely she'd have been in touch with him too.

I also felt ridiculously cheered that she had asked if I wanted to join in her investigation. I'd worried over recent years that our relationship was becoming diluted, that we were drifting apart, but this seemed to be a validation of our friendship. And also, she must think there was something I could contribute to helping Nate Ogden. I was excited and intrigued.

Normally, I'm very good about not using the phone while I'm driving. It can ping and blip away at me with new texts and voicemails as much as it wants. Aware how vital a clean driving licence is to my business, I wait until I'm sedately parked before checking them.

But something told me this particular ping was important. One-handed, and illegally, I checked the text. It was from Ben. It just read: 'I'm not so good, Ma.'

There was only one possible response.

I unplugged the satnav, turned back towards Chichester, and drove in a way that was certainly a threat to my clean licence.

# THIRTEEN

There's something in my life I try not to talk about. That doesn't mean that I don't think about it. The memory is with me every day, and most nights too. Everyone close to me knows what happened. Probably a lot of people not close to me at all also know. And I do talk about it sometimes. People in the healing professions – people like Hilary – are constantly telling me I should talk about it more often, telling me that it would help – but my instinct is not to.

It's the reason for the choking dream, the one I don't get so often now, thank God.

And it's the reason I had no choice but to abandon the quest for Nate Ogden and drive straight home after Ben's text.

Obviously, it's to do with Jools's and Ben's father. My husband. Oliver.

He was a cartoonist. I met him a long time after Philip and I split up. Well, Philip and I didn't actually split up, we just kind of drifted apart. He was getting increasingly caught up in his medical studies, and I was kind of drifting around in the Chichester area, where I'd been brought up. I had finished school and was contemplating university. I supposed that I would end up doing an English degree somewhere. I'd always liked words and loved reading. Still do, when I get time.

My A levels were good enough, but I didn't want to go straight back into full-time education. I thought if I took a year out – working locally, serving in shops, behind bars – I might emerge with a clearer idea of what I wanted to do with my life. Or who I was, perhaps? I was still living with Fleur – well, that is to say in Fleur's house. She wasn't there much. I couldn't afford to live anywhere else – and that kind of worked OK, so long as I gave her all my attention when she was there.

I did go up to spend a few weekends with Philip, but neither of us was that interested in extending the relationship. The sex, which had started out very exciting and new, had become a bit predictable. Philip was very in and in-jokey with all his fellow medical students and I . . . well, I didn't really know where I was. Not unhappy, just unsure where I wanted to go next. Drifting. Philip and I agreed to part, and I don't think either of us was too bothered by the decision.

But it did make me restless. There was nothing to keep me in Chichester. Nothing to keep me in England, really.

So, I thought I'd take a kind of gap year. Travel. I started in the USA, worked myself down to South America, ended up in Australia. On the way, I had a sequence of very short and unsatisfactory jobs. Also, shorter and even more unsatisfactory relationships. Then, in Sydney, I met someone who I thought might go the distance. The one gap year became five. I got a regular job in a bar in the Rocks area.

I had very occasional contact with Fleur during that period. Every month or so, I would make a duty phone call, when she would tell me how wonderfully well her career and love life were going. She never asked about mine. Never tried to call me either.

The man in Sydney didn't go the distance. All I wanted to do with distance then was to put as much between him and me as possible. So, I came back to England. To Chichester.

I could still have applied for university but the moment seemed to have passed.

Fleur made no secret of the fact that my return to her home was inconvenient. She had recently married her second husband and didn't want anything to disturb their short-lived romantic idyll. I rented a small flat, got various local jobs, working in shops and bars, and wondered what the hell was going to happen next.

I got back in touch with some of my still unattached school-friends and drank too much in their company. 'Ladette culture' was much spoken of at the time, and I got into a cycle of rather joyless excess. I did not anticipate any more excitements in my life.

I wasn't depressed, just numb and pissed off, really.

I met Oliver when I was working for a while in Waterstone's. He'd got a book of cartoons out, called *Major Cock-Ups*, based on a series he'd done for a daily newspaper about the then prime minister. It was meant to clean up in the Christmas Funnies book market (it didn't), and the publishers had organized a series of signings. Chichester Waterstone's was one of the stops on his tour. The city was thick with snow and very few of its well-heeled citizens wanted to leave their central heating for a book signing.

After Oliver had done his well-rehearsed (and very funny) routine and signed a few (very few) books, a bunch of us went out for a drink, and it ended up with just him and me, alone and pretty pissed in the pub. The snow made us feel comfortably isolated, cocooned from the icy world outside.

Oliver was meant to be catching a train back to London round nine o'clock, but he missed that one. He kept looking at his watch and commenting on the other ones he'd missed. And if there was more snow, would the trains even be running? Eventually, the bar staff had to kick us out at closing time. He reckoned there was still a train he could catch. I never did find out whether there was or not.

Outside the pub, he kissed me formally on both cheeks and asked for my phone number. I gave it, never expecting to hear from him again, and Oliver reeled off towards the station.

He left me in a state of precarious ecstasy. Drunk, for a start. And bitterly cold beside the ice-covered Market Cross. But also, warmed by the unshifting focus of Oliver's brown eyes and mesmerized by his talk. I'm sure they were all practised anecdotes – I came to hear them a good few times over the ensuing years – but I had never been in the company of anyone who'd made me laugh so much.

During the next few days I settled into a kind of rueful resignation and thought of all the reasons why there was no possibility of a relationship between me and Oliver ever happening – or, if it did – ever working.

He was older than me, for a start. Probably at least fifteen years older. And from his talk, it was clear there had been quite a lot of women in his life. At what level of seriousness those relationships had been, I had no means of knowing. Nor did I know whether he was in one of them at that moment. Fewer men wore wedding rings back then, and I thought Oliver was probably the kind of guy who wouldn't have worn one, anyway.

I reconciled myself to the fact that I was just one in a string of girls working in bookshops, over whom Oliver had spread his minor celebrity charm for an evening. Out of my league.

Then he rang me.

I'm not going to describe what being in love's like. People who've been there know, and I don't want to make people who haven't jealous. All I need to say is that Oliver and I worked.

There were problems, of course. My mother was appalled by the age difference, and even more appalled when Oliver was revealed to have two divorces behind him – though what right Fleur Bonnier had to get on a high horse about morality in relationships seemed to me to have a pot-and-kettle element to it. She also told me that his fractured love life was a sign of instability of character. I was initially pretty shocked by the revelations too, but I was in love with him, so for me their importance diminished. For Fleur, who was far from being in love with him, they became more important. Though I think her main objection to my having a successful relationship was the thought of her being upstaged.

The only thing that worried me about Oliver was the frequent occurrence of his dark moods. Suddenly, in the middle of his customary wisecracking, he would go quiet. It was very difficult to talk to him at such moments. The darkness might last for a few hours, a couple of days, then he would suddenly grin, say, 'Sorry about that', and be back to the man I had first met in Waterstone's.

With the glibness of youth, I didn't worry about this too much. Being in love gave me enormous confidence in the power of that love. So, Oliver had low moods from time to time. What of it? My love was strong enough to heal and protect him.

At first, I continued to work at Waterstone's in Chichester and spent as much time as I could with Oliver on his Regent's Canal narrowboat. Over a few months, I gave up the job and moved in. I didn't need to contribute to the household income.

Those were good years for Oliver. His stock as a cartoonist was high. The Major Cock-Up strip was in a London evening paper every weekday, and was also syndicated to a lot of overseas publications. Though Oliver admitted to being very bad at managing money, there was no doubt there was a lot of it coming in.

With a change of government, obviously the Major cartoons were out. This could have been a disaster for Oliver, but in fact it proved a blessing. Because he thought of something better. He adjusted to the new administration by starting a new strip about a children's cuddly toy called Teddy Blair. This proved to be even more successful than Major Cock-Ups.

The demands of the strip meant a very stressful start to each day. Oliver would wake at five and walk down to King's Cross to pick up all the daily newspapers. Then he'd wrestle through them for a couple of hours until he'd got three potential ideas for the day's sequence. By eight o'clock he'd have rung his editor to spell out the jokes. The editor would pick the one to go with, and Oliver would spend the next couple of hours drawing it up properly, before ringing for a cab to take the finished artwork to the newspaper office (no email back then).

It was a punishing routine, but once the material was in the cab, the rest of the day was his own. So, by half past ten, Oliver would be having his first drink of the day. Red wine, always red wine. If I was there, by eleven we'd be in bed, making love.

Compared to my earlier fumblings – and experiences with Philip – I couldn't believe how good sex was with Oliver. I think it was the first time I fully understood the meaning of the word 'consensual'. There was no competition, no one was trying to score points over anyone, it was just a process of mutual exploration and pleasure. Skin on skin. You know when it feels right.

Fleur accused me of deliberately getting pregnant with Jools, and though I hotly denied the charge, there may have been a grain of truth in it. I certainly wasn't upset when I missed my period. I think I thought that everything was so perfect, having a child together would bind us even closer. I thought I could encompass Oliver with love, protect him against his dark moments, create the kind of nurturing family atmosphere that neither of us had ever had the pleasure of enjoying.

I had certainly not anticipated his reaction to the news. I held back till I'd missed a couple of periods and done a pregnancy test. I was very joyful when I told him.

He wasn't. It was the first time he ever shouted at me. And it all came out. His family's history of depression, his own battles with negativity and self-loathing from his teens onwards. His encounters with psychiatrists and medication. His despair when nothing seemed to work.

He also spoke in more detail about his previous relationships and how few of the women could cope with the volatility caused by his depression. He then got on to the two marriages. One had ended because the wife finally said, 'I didn't sign up for this to become a psychiatric nurse.'

And the issue that broke the other marriage was children. The wife wanted them; Oliver didn't. I'll never forget the words he said to me, newly pregnant. 'People like me should never have children. It's irresponsible to risk passing this illness down to another generation.'

Oliver wanted me to abort the baby. I refused. I argued that any child we produced would have at least half of its genetic inheritance from me. And I had never felt more positive in my life. My good blood would flush away his bad blood.

The pregnancy would have been a happy time for me, were it not for the extremes of mood that I saw Oliver going through. I'd never met a depressive before, and myself had not suffered from anything worse than bad temper. Those moods of mine came on furiously and fast and vanished as quickly. I always found anger therapeutic. Oliver almost never expressed anger against anyone else. He turned it inward, inflicted the pain on himself.

I got to recognize the signs. He would go quiet; he would avoid eye contact. He'd go through patches of hardly sleeping at all, alternating those with sleep so deep as almost to be comatose. Sometimes I literally had to drag him out of bed and sit him behind his drawing board. I'd go through the papers with him, never pointing out subjects that I thought might make good strips but helping him to find them on his own.

Then, depression subsumed in concentration, he would put in a couple of manic hours to produce the artwork. Whatever his mood, he never missed a deadline. How he achieved that before he had me there in bed to nudge him into action, I did not know. Perhaps I didn't want to know. Because the answer was probably that he *had* had someone else there in bed to nudge him into action.

The pregnancy was blessedly uncomplicated. Towards the end of it, Oliver became positively excited about the prospect of being a father. He insisted on being in the Labour Ward with me, and I'd never seen such radiant happiness in his face than when he first held Jools (then Juliet) in his arms.

He never put it into words, but I think it was the first time in his life that Oliver had felt undiluted love. From hints and half-stories he told me, all of his adult relationships had been complex. The one he had with me was probably the simplest, but even there he found and talked endlessly about imagined problems. If I hadn't been so convinced of the rightness of our being together, I don't think we would have survived.

His love for our baby, though, was instinctive and – to use a word later to feature a lot in my life – uncluttered.

The first year of Juliet's life was one of the happiest of my own. The narrowboat was an idyllic home for a relatively immobile baby. Very gradually, without upsetting the way Oliver liked things to be, I cleared the chaos in which he had grown to live. I suppose the boat was my first exercise in decluttering. I changed the curtains for something brighter, then moved on to the bed linen and towels. For his forty-third birthday, I had some of Oliver's original artwork framed, and hung those on the walls. I ensured that there were always flowers on the tables. I added, I suppose, what, even in these enlightened times, would be called 'a woman's touch'.

Oliver's work was going well. The Teddy Blair strip was syndicated in more newspapers, and its success led to him being commissioned to create another daily cartoon series. This, Riq and Raq (short for Raquel), was about the hazards for a young couple negotiating urban life with a small child. It was about us, actually. Because it was based more on domestic trends than on the day's news, the pressure was less. Oliver could actually stockpile strips. On a good day, having delivered his Teddy Blair, he could produce half a dozen Riq and Raqs. Then he'd take a few days off to spend playing with Juliet, an activity of which neither of them ever seemed to tire.

Developing technology also made Oliver's work easier. After a shaky start, he soon got into drawing straight on to the computer, which made last-minute changes much easier. And email meant that he no longer had to send his precious sole copy of the artwork off in a taxi.

To my surprise, he allowed me to take over the management of our finances. I taught myself how to do it – and the experience of running that very small business certainly helped when I set up SpaceWoman. It also made me realize just how much Oliver was making. Previously, he knew he had money, but was never quite sure where it was. Everything went into his current account. And twice a year, there'd be a panic when the tax demand arrived.

I reorganized that, separating our domestic account from the business one and adding a savings account to deal with tax bills. Later, I made the business into a limited company. Riq and Raq was getting syndicated extensively by then, and there was a lot more coming in. We had a very nice lifestyle.

Given his two previous experiences of the state, I was very careful never to mention the subject of marriage. But, to my delight, when Juliet was about six months old, Oliver asked me to marry him. His approach was characteristically apologetic. He said that he hadn't really got anything to offer any woman, that he had a bad track record with relationships, that the depression was liable to return at any time, but would I consider screwing up my life on a permanent basis by becoming his wife?

I was ecstatic, envisioning all the church and white dress imagery which I had always pretended didn't interest me. But it soon became clear that Oliver didn't want anything too public. His first wedding had had all the ecclesiastical bells and whistles. The second had been a smaller-scale event at a registry office, but with everyone dressing up and a reception at a swish hotel afterwards. Ours he wanted to be even lower key than that. Registry office again, but only a couple of friends there as witnesses.

I can't pretend I wasn't disappointed, but I swallowed down the feelings, unexpressed. I was, after all, about to be married to the man I adored. That was all that mattered.

Fleur Bonnier's disappointment was more overtly expressed.
A big wedding was, for her, just another stage to dominate. And
not even to be invited to her only child's wedding was, to her
mind, a slap in the face.

I mitigated the offence by organizing a dinner in a restaurant
soon after, for just me and Oliver, my mother and her current
paramour, a rather wooden actor who had had a small part in
*Blake's 7*. Since Fleur not only went on about not being invited
to the registry office, but also had got to the snappy, coming-
up-to-the-end-of-the-relationship stage with her lover, it wasn't
a great evening.

But Oliver and I were married. We had Juliet. That was all
that mattered.

I won't say the depression disappeared during those early years,
but it was better. Oliver's dark moods didn't last so long. Most
of the time he was on a pretty even keel. Even at his lowest, his
devotion to Juliet gave him something to live for.

I remember some people asked if I felt jealous about my
husband's overwhelming love for our daughter, and I could
honestly say that I never did. We were all part of that love.

Oliver told me many times that the depression hadn't gone
away, never would go away for good. It was always lurking there,
ready to ambush him at the least expected moment.

His illness wasn't the result of some trauma, like the form
suffered by 'people who write books about depression', he
always said dismissively. They're always gobsmacked by some
adult shock or bereavement which had sent them into a downward
spiral. 'With me,' he repeated, 'it's always been there.' He reckoned it was genetic, 'like having red hair'. His mother had suffered
badly at a period when the subject wasn't mentioned, and she'd
had to 'pretend everything was all right all the time'. The tension
between how she was feeling and how she had to appear to be
feeling was, according to Oliver, what caused her death in her
early fifties. His father, a shadowy figure rarely mentioned, was
also dead.

What brought about Oliver's next collapse, when Juliet was
nearly two, was the issue of moving house. The charms of narrowboat living palled when there was an extremely active toddler

around. There wasn't enough room, for a start, and although we had put protective railings and netting all around the boat, I was still in a perpetual state of anxiety about her falling off. London life, so seductive for an untrammelled couple, was less appealing with all the paraphernalia, the troop movements of buggies and folding cots. I wanted to move back to the south coast.

My first mention of the idea knocked him sideways. He'd never owned any property. The narrowboat, like all his previous homes had been, was rented. The thought of commitment to a mortgage, like the thought of having a child, started a cycle of imagined inadequacies and self-loathing. He kept saying, 'Suppose we can't pay it? Suppose the house has to be repossessed? Suppose I had a complete breakdown and couldn't work? We'd be letting Juliet down horribly.'

My intimate knowledge of our financial position, and a bit of research into the housing market, had reassured me that, without stretching ourselves to dangerous limits, we could well afford a nice family house in the Chichester area. And Oliver's income from the cartoons was still rising every year. But, when he was so far down in depression, he was immune to rational argument.

It was a tough one, but I persevered. As I knew I would, I had to do all the paperwork and negotiation on my own. It took a lot of persuasion to get Oliver to sign the necessary documentation. All he could see ahead was failure and disaster.

I found the right place, a four-bedroomed house with a garage and large garden, in Funtington, a village some five miles north of Chichester. There was a pub, a nursery and a primary school close enough to walk to. Oliver really tried to share my enthusiasm for the project, but the depression crippled his efforts.

The shift in his attitude was not as quick as it had been with Juliet's birth. But, over the first few months of living in the new house, his fears were allayed. None of the disastrous scenarios he had envisaged actually worked out. Again, developing technology helped. Being out of London did not cut off his political sources. Ideas germinated and flourished. People still wanted to employ him. More people wanted to employ him. Emails flew back and forth, commissions started to come in from other countries, including America. To everyone except himself, Oliver Curtis was a major success.

And, gradually, he relaxed into his new surroundings. He even got the confidence to do something he'd never done before – and turn down work he didn't want to do.

My happiness was complete when Oliver, off his own bat, suggested something which I'd been on the verge of mentioning for months. He said that we should have another child.

Ben was born nine months to the day after the suggestion was made. From the start, he was adorable. Juliet was so proud of her new brother and loved him just as much as his parents did.

And, as Juliet and Ben grew older, I would show them the framed cartoons in the hall and tell them what a clever Daddy they had.

The years that followed, with Oliver working from home, sharing the upbringing of our two children in the Funtington house, were the happiest of my life.

# FOURTEEN

When I first found out about Oliver's depression, my youthful, optimistic, can-do attitude made me determined to find a cure for it. I read a lot of books on the subject ('depression porn', he called them) and, as the internet developed, looked up more and more stuff online.

He didn't discourage me. He monitored my efforts with a kind of weary patience. He had tried most recommended solutions and, though some had brought respite to the condition, none had eradicated it. After a few months, the depression always returned.

But it wasn't there all the time. From the moment of our first encounter, Oliver remained the funniest person I have ever met. The children soon caught on to his sense of humour, and our house rang with frequent laughter. I don't think that, during their childhood years, they were aware of his illness. All right, Dad sometimes went quiet for a while, but such behaviour was just another mystery of adult life.

He, on the other hand, worried continuously about them. Were they showing signs of depression? Had the dire prediction, which had prevented him from having children before, been realized? I was so genuinely unafraid of this outcome that it did not cause me a moment's anxiety. Juliet and Ben were just like other kids. Yes, they had moods and threw tantrums – usually when they didn't get their own way – but showed no signs of anything that wasn't normal (how much Oliver and I argued about the definition of that word).

Looking back on events in life, it is often difficult to pinpoint why they happened. Rarely is there one single factor responsible. Effects arise out of a tangle of causes.

I was busy and perhaps didn't notice the more permanent shift in Oliver's mood. While the children were there, I had got quite involved in the local primary. I did a lot of one-to-one reading with the slower pupils. We were well enough off for me to do that as a volunteer.

But the hours mounted up and, after Juliet moved on to the comprehensive in Chichester, I found myself involved in more and more school activities. I liked the fact that I was near Ben. I'd see him in the course of the day, smiling, laughing with his mates, half proud and half embarrassed that his mum was on school premises.

Oliver's work wasn't going so well. Obviously, the topicality of the Teddy Blair strip was long gone. Riq and Raq survived longer, but that kind of social satire dates quickly, and soon younger cartoonists, more in tune with the contemporary zeitgeist, took over the slot. Oliver Curtis was still a name to be reckoned with in the world of cartoonists. He was often called on for book illustration and one-off commissions, but the regular bread-and-butter continuity of work had gone.

Oliver blamed himself for this. Whatever he had once had, he had lost it. Maybe he'd never had anything in the first place. Maybe he'd just got lucky by being in the right place at the right time. He was in his fifties. There were few comebacks in the cartoon world for people of that age.

I argued these points with him endlessly until, frankly, I got quite bored with them. It is very tiring telling someone so often that the apocalypse is not about to arrive.

I reassured him about our financial situation, too. Though I say it myself, I had managed our money well. The mortgage on the house had been paid off early, and I had made some shrewd investments in shares and pensions. I kept assuring Oliver that, even if he never earned anything else, we wouldn't have to change our lifestyle. Such arguments did not comfort him. He saw the diminution of work offers as his own fault.

His relationship with Juliet also changed. Inevitably, when she started having periods and turning to spotty bolshiness, she could no longer be Daddy's little girl. Like most teenagers, she turned against her parents. For me, with whom there had always been a spikiness, that was not such a big deal. But for Oliver, Jools's unwillingness to be hugged was devastating.

I have relived the moment so many times, trying and failing to make sense of it, wondering what I could have done to change the outcome, but I have found no answers.

In retrospect, I should have noticed that Oliver had seemed perkier the few days before. But I was cheered rather than worried by that. I thought he was at last coming out of his latest, long, persistent depression.

It was lunchtime. I'd spent the morning doing my remedial reading at the primary school. I waved to Ben as I left the playground. He grinned at me. Juliet was at school in Chichester.

The unanswering silence in the house when I called out told me something was wrong.

I found Oliver in the garage. He'd very efficiently attached a hosepipe to the exhaust, fed it back into the car and switched on the engine. The fumes in the enclosed space choked me too, my first experience of the choking that was to haunt so many dreams. That terrible smell of petrol.

Oliver was dead.

He hadn't left a note. There was no need to. He knew I'd know the reason. He just couldn't fight the self-hatred any more.

# FIFTEEN

That was, of course, why I rushed home after receiving Ben's message, 'I'm not so good, Ma.' Finding out who killed Kerry Tallis became a very minor consideration when my son needed me.

Whether it was the trauma of his father's suicide that triggered it, or whether it was just genetic ('like having red hair', as I know Oliver would have argued), Ben soon started to show depressive tendencies.

His sister reacted the other way. Juliet constructed a carapace around herself, through which she did not allow emotions to penetrate. She became Jools, apparently shallow, flippant, even glib. Though she was present on many family occasions, she ceased to be an active participant in family life. She turned against me even more and, perhaps just to annoy me, cosied up to Fleur. She deliberately went against my green principles and became a major consumer of everything. She developed the unassailable persona which was later to make her such a success in the London fashion world.

Her father's suicide ended her dependence on me.

Whereas, with Ben . . .

He adored Oliver and was just on the cusp of adolescence when his father died. He went into his first major catatonic depression about three months later. I had to collect him from school, unresponding, locked into his own darkness.

He had to have time out. I was obviously in a bad state myself, but I've never had a depressive bone in my body, and maybe dealing with Ben's traumas gave me something outside myself to focus on. I consulted doctors and psychologists. Appalled by the waiting time for NHS consultations, I went private. Ben was questioned and probed and medicated. And for a time he'd be 'normal' (whatever that means).

Then the Oliver pattern would repeat itself. I've lost count of the number of times I've had to rescue Ben from school and, later, university. He's doing graphic design – and he's bloody good at it, genetics again – at Nottingham Trent. The areas he's particularly interested in are animation (all done on the computer now) and typography. He once confided in me that his long-term ambition is to design a new font that becomes as famous as Baskerville or Helvetica. He stores all kinds of examples on his laptop and is constantly accessing old newspaper archives to check out their printing styles. Ben is, needless to say, like all of his generation, extremely proficient with computers.

Very promising student then. Talented, creative, inventive. But already he's had to start the course again, after a major breakdown in his first year.

Mothers, it's said, never cease to worry about their children. With Ben, given the family history, my anxiety is on a different scale.

Oliver's death meant we had to make some practical changes to our lives. Though I'd been good with money, we couldn't keep on the Funtington house without any new income coming in. Besides, I could never relax in the place after what had happened there. Nor could I bear to buy another house with a garage. So, we got the place in Chichester.

Had to get rid of a lot of furniture. Good training for when I started SpaceWoman. I kept the cartoons of Oliver's that I'd had framed, but I didn't put any on display. They stayed in the cupboard under the stairs. I wouldn't be strong enough for a long time to hang any of them where I could see them.

The few people I've talked to about Oliver's death have all asked me if I feel guilty about it. The answer, perhaps surprisingly, is no. Oh, sure, I have guilt about practical things – that I wasn't there when it happened, that I didn't come back to the house an hour earlier. But I do not feel personal guilt. I know that Oliver didn't kill himself because of anything I did. Indeed, being with me probably saved him from doing the deed much earlier. I do understand that much about depression. Oliver suffered from an illness that never fully went away.

But knowing that doesn't stop me from missing him every day of my life.

As I hurtled the Yeti back towards home and Ben, I berated myself for not recognizing the signs. My study of the subject had taught me that depressives very rarely commit suicide when they're at their lowest. At such times, their energy and initiative are so drained that they are incapable of organizing anything. But, as they emerge from the depression – particularly if it's been a long one – then they feel capable of taking positive action. And of ensuring that they never have to undergo such pain again.

It was what had happened with Oliver. He'd been remarkably chipper in the days before he killed himself. And when I last spoke to Ben, I now realized, he too had sounded dangerously perky.

My son was sitting at the kitchen table. There was a glass and a half-empty bottle of whisky in front of him. And, neatly piled up, about ten boxes of paracetamol. The government's restricting of the contents to sixteen was probably a well-intentioned safety strategy, but any potential suicide is capable of stockpiling.

I looked at Ben. He evaded my eye. I looked at the paracetamol. 'Have you?'

'No,' he said. 'Not yet.' Then he dissolved into tears. 'I'm sorry, Ma.'

It had happened before. It was my nightmare. Jools knew about her brother's suicidal tendency. I think Hilary probably suspected it. I didn't advertise the details. I didn't want people talking about 'cries for help'. I would have hit them if they had.

Given the family history, I had taken Ben to any number of doctors and psychiatrists over the years. He had been put on all kinds of medication, and he was very good about taking it. He knew the pain his condition caused me. He fought against it. No one could have fought harder. And he was determined to live an independent life.

But always the depression returned. Like Oliver, Ben sometimes wanted to kill himself. He even used his father's expression for the inherited illness. 'It's like having red hair.'

\*  \*  \*

I never knew. If I'd arrived half an hour later, would I have found him dead? I've asked that question so many times. Of course, it hasn't always been me who's found him in that state. Schoolfriends, university friends, passers-by on bridges, someone has always got there on time to stop the final destructive act.

As I said, there are few people I've ever talked to about Ben's situation, apart from the medical professionals who have dealt with him over the years. Hilary sometimes, she at least understands the issues of mental illness. I never raise the subject with Fleur, but often she brings it up. She doesn't put her view into words, but the implication goes back to her reservations about my marrying Oliver. She told me he was unstable, but did I listen? The corollary of that is that Ben's condition is my fault. But then my mother has spent her life trying to convince me that everything is my fault.

I certainly will not allow her to blame Ben. I get atavistically maternal and defensive if Fleur talks about 'drawing attention to himself'. I find that particularly rich coming from someone who has spent her entire life doing that very thing.

Like his father, Ben suffers from an illness. He hates that fact as much as I do. But his moments of despair are absolutely genuine. He never makes stuff up.

After one of his thwarted suicide attempts, there are two ways he can go. Either he turns very listless and lethargic, sleeping for whole days and nights. Or he becomes manic.

My son in manic mode is very charismatic. Like his father, he can be remarkably witty, ideas spinning out of him, unlikely connections being snapped together. I can fully understand why, at such times, he is devastatingly attractive to women. I can also understand why his inability to sustain that mood mean that all of his relationships have, sooner or later, fallen apart.

That evening, the one when I had been diverted from the search for Nate Ogden, Ben was manic. The whisky was talking a bit too.

'I'm wasting your time,' he said. 'You're busy. You were going somewhere.'

'Yes, but it doesn't matter,' I said, suppressing the powerful curiosity Hilary's text had fired in me. 'I'll stay here with you.'

'No need. I've been a naughty boy. Rap over the knuckles.' With one large gesture he swept up the paracetamol packets into his arms and dumped them in the pedal-bin. 'No danger now. Get on with your life, Ma.'

'You know I'm not going to leave you tonight, Ben.'

'I'm fine.'

'Yes?'

'Yes. Ready to do battle. With my trusty broadsword to defeat the Giant Depression. My strength is as the strength of ten because my heart is pure! Well, not entirely pure, perhaps, but then that's difficult for my generation with so much porn readily available.'

Inevitably, I found myself laughing. Ben quoting Tennyson, for God's sake! What had got into him? At such times, he was so like Oliver. He had the same feverish sparkle in his eye. And, for me, laughing was better than crying.

'So, look, here I am, a knight errant looking for an errand for the night. What can I do to aid you, fair damsel in distress?'

'I'm fine. Don't need any aid.'

'But you do. Everyone needs aid. Here I am, spurred and booted on my gift horse. Don't look me in the mouth. And, talking of mouths, Ma, yours might be less dry if it were irrigated by a glass of whisky.'

Not waiting for agreement, he leapt up to get another glass and filled it for me. He raised his to clink. 'To putting recent events behind us!'

'I'll drink to that,' I said.

I did. The spirit burnt comfortingly down my throat.

'So, tell me, Ma, what was the quest from which I distracted you? Which particular made-in-China replica of the Holy Grail were you searching for this evening?'

'I was looking for someone who might be a murderer,' I replied.

Ben was instantly hooked and wanted more details. I could think of no reason to deny them to him. The entire nation knew about Kerry Tallis's death. The disappearance of Nate Ogden had also been publicized in a way that implied a connection between the two events. There were photographs of both of them all over the papers. The only new information I'd be giving Ben would be how I came to be involved in the situation. And he already knew about my discovering Kerry's corpse.

My son's eyes sparkled as I came to the end of my narration. 'And you don't think you should leave me alone tonight, Ma?'

'I'm not going to leave you alone tonight, Ben.'

'No? Good.'

'What do you mean?'

'I mean I'm going to come with you. We're going to search for the murderer together.'

At the time, that seemed to me like a very good idea.

'You're mad,' I said.

'I know,' said Ben, with his father's grin. 'Lucky I'm not suicidal, though, isn't it?'

# SIXTEEN

As the Yeti approached the destination entered into the satnav, I realized why the postcode seemed familiar. It was familiar because I had been there before. On Friday, the day that I had found Kerry's body. My headlights caught the hanging sign. Walnut Farm. The empty property I'd been summoned to earlier that same day.

It was definitively dark by the time we got there. Moonless, clouds overhead. Ben switched on his phone light, while I got the torch out of the boot.

The beam moved across the dusty windows of the untended frontage. There were no lights from inside. But this time, when I tried the front-door handle, it gave inwards.

'This is *fun*,' Ben murmured, close behind me.

In the hallway the torch beam revealed faded wallpaper, here and there torn and sagging. Though by origin a stable or workshop, the building had been converted into living accommodation. But the work was rough and ready. The place couldn't be dignified by the description of 'barn conversion'. And it looked as though no one had lived there for a long time.

The left-hand door off the hall revealed a kitchen. Dusty sink, empty shelves, it hadn't been used for years.

Through the door opposite was a toilet, bowl cracked and grey, chain to overhead cistern broken, a smell of damp and dust.

The remaining door opened on to a large space, twice as high as the hallway. This had presumably been the main part of the building, with space enough to house carts and farm machinery. As my torchlight scoped upwards, between the struts and rafters were revealed the undersides of the roofing slates.

From a cross beam at the far end hung what I somehow knew I would find there. The heavy body of Nate Ogden.

The noose tied around the rafter and constricting his angled neck was made of orange polypropylene. On the floor beneath him, on its side, lay the chair which he must have kicked away.

I, as transfixed as the corpse was, kept the torch beam on the still body, cursing myself for having brought Ben into this scene of tragedy.

But I had underestimated my son. Suddenly masterful, he stepped forward towards the scene of the crime. 'Have you got your tape measure, Ma?' he asked.

Wordlessly, I reached into my pocket and handed across the ribbon of fabric. I watched, fascinated, as Ben checked the distance between the dead man's dangling feet and the floor. I still watched, immobile, as he measured the height of the chair lying on its side.

'There's no way he could have got so high from standing on the chair,' said my son. 'Someone strung him up there. He was murdered.'

He's bright, my son.

# SEVENTEEN

Of course, it had to be the police again. Of course, it didn't take them long to identify me as the woman who had discovered the corpse in the Hargood Estate flat. Nor long to come to the view that such a coincidence was possibly grounds for suspicion. To be the first person to find a murder victim was one thing. To then be the first person to discover the corpse of the man who was suspected of murdering her . . . well, that was, to put it at the mildest, unusual.

As on the previous occasion, the initial response to our mobile call to the police was a couple of uniforms in a Panda car. Though a summons went through pretty quickly to Detective Inspector Prendergast, there was a good hour of waiting around till he appeared. We sat in the Yeti. The sidekick this time wasn't Prasad. A black woman with a Caribbean rhythm to her voice, whose name I didn't retain. What is this habit I have of not registering the names of police officers? A result of stress, probably. Most things are.

The only good thing about the questioning I underwent was that Ben was with me. Since we had found Nate Ogden's body together, there was no point in separating us. This was good for me. Not only did I have his moral support, I also knew where he was. I was worried about how he might react to what we'd just encountered. Didn't know whether Ben had ever even seen a dead body before. But what he'd witnessed at Walnut Farm seemed to have left him on a high, almost manic. I knew that mood could not last for ever. And I was fearful of what would happen when it shifted.

Among the many other thoughts flooding my brain was the permanent undercurrent of worry about Ben. What should I do after this latest manifestation of his illness? Back to the GP to try yet another change of medication? Back to one of the many psychiatrists we'd consulted over the years? Please, not back to one of those grim mental institutions in which he had at times been incarcerated. With these thoughts recurred the bleak feeling that nothing was going to change his personality in a permanent way. He would always be a depressive.

To the police, Ben showed no sign of his recent trauma. I was proud of the way he dealt with them. He was polite and accurate in his answers, the perfect witness. He was also discreet. He made no mention of his views about how Nate Ogden had died. Let the police reach their own conclusions in their own good time.

It was inevitable that, in my replies, I would mention Hilary. It was, after all, through her agency that I had gone to Walnut Farm. And, as Detective Inspector Prendergast patiently questioned me, I realized how suspicious her actions might sound to someone who didn't know and trust her the way I did.

It's dark again. And I'm strapped in, belt diagonally across my chest, tight over my thighs.

And again, though I breathe, there is no sustenance in the air. What I gulp down is vile and metallic. I feel it clogging my lungs. I feel it evaporating all the saliva in my throat. I feel it choking me.

I know what Oliver felt in the final moments of his life.

And I wake up. The clock radio reproaches me with the fact that it's only 12.43 a.m.

I go to check on Ben. I'd given him a Zopiclone. He is sleeping deeply, breathing with that easy rhythm which I have listened to and warmed to from the moment of his birth.

Sometimes I cannot believe how much I love him.

# EIGHTEEN

I did get back to sleep for a few twitchy hours but woke irreversibly at 6.17. I lay there trying to think what I could do about Ben. He was a grown man. I didn't want to mollycoddle him. And yet I had to protect him from himself. I couldn't spend every moment of my life monitoring his moods, though. There were other demands on my time. I had to keep SpaceWoman running. And, increasingly, I was intrigued by the two murders in which I had inadvertently become involved. I've never thought of myself as an amateur sleuth, but I do have my fair share of natural curiosity. More than my fair share, some would say.

Round 6.55, when I was about to switch on the *Today* programme, I had an idea. It was something I'd contemplated before, but never followed through on. I knew he kept early hours, so I rang straight through to Dodge.

He sounded pleased to hear me. He always seems more relaxed on the phone, once he knows who he's talking to. Though he can't look anyone in the eye in face-to-face encounters, phone calls remove that problem.

'Dodge, I have a favour to ask you.'

'No problem. What is it?'

I had never talked to him openly about Ben's mental health, but Dodge seemed to have intuited that there was a problem. In the same way, I've never talked to him openly about Oliver's suicide, but he seems to know about that too. So, I chose my words with care. 'Look, I've got a large, strong son loafing around at home . . . university vacation and all that . . . and I just wondered if you might need some help with anything today . . .?'

As I'd hoped, Dodge understood exactly what I meant. And also, why I was framing my request in such a roundabout way. 'In fact, the timing's rather good, Ellen. Yesterday I picked up a load of old wooden vats from a brewery that's closing down. I have plans for recycling them . . .'

'Into what?' I couldn't help asking.

He chuckled. 'That remains to be seen. I often have to look at something I salvage for a long time before I decide what it can become. Anyway, they're bloody big buggers. I could get them off the van myself, but it'd take time. With two of us, the job'd be a lot easier. So yes, I could find work for a large, strong son.'

He's brilliantly intuitive, Dodge. He knew exactly what I meant. He fully understood that I didn't want Ben to be alone. That's the kind of understanding, I'm sure, which makes him such a success with the work he does at ReProgramme. Someone who's been as low in his own life as Dodge has is never going to be judgemental about other people's problems.

I woke Ben, which was not an easy task, because he was still muzzy from the Zopiclone. But when he did come to his senses, it was clear that the manic mood was still on him. He was bright to the point of brittleness. Which is always a bit scary for me.

He welcomed the proposal that he should help Dodge and said, 'But, before that, Ma, I'm going to cook you the biggest Full English Breakfast that has ever passed your lips.'

It was so enormous that at least I knew I wouldn't have to look for anything at lunchtime. I dropped Ben off at Dodge's and caught up on visits I'd been neglecting.

It was less than a week since I'd last seen Queenie, but I still felt guilty. She looked thinner than ever and I wondered if she'd eaten anything on the intervening days. As I admired the cat illustration she'd shown me a hundred times before, and listened to her shock at what the weather girl on *South Today* had been wearing, I made sure she had one of the Hobnobs I'd brought with me.

The fact that I only listened with half an ear to tales of her cats' antics made me feel even guiltier. I was on tenterhooks. I felt certain Detective Inspector Prendergast would be back in touch. It was only a matter of time.

I was also desperately curious to know what Hilary had said to the investigating police. They were bound to have talked to her.

The failure of concentration continued when I went to see Ashleigh and Zak. Again, it was less than a week since I'd last seen her, but it was amazing how much rubbish had built up in the flat in that short time. There was also the ominous news that

Ashleigh had got into a row with one of her neighbours over the weekend. Inevitably, about playing her music too loud. From her account, she clearly hadn't apologized. Instead, she'd snapped back, which had only exacerbated the situation. The neighbour had said she was going to complain to the housing authority.

Again, I felt I should be listening more attentively to what Ashleigh said. I should be coming up with solutions, offering to intervene on her behalf. But my mind was elsewhere.

It was while I was with her, getting on for ten in the morning, that I received a text. Making my excuses, I hurried out with indecent haste and was checking my phone the minute I was through the door.

Hilary. Asking me to call. I did.

'Where are you?' I asked.

'Home. The police have just been questioning me.'

'Prendergast?'

'Yes.'

'How was it?'

'We need to talk,' was all she said by way of reply.

'Buon Caffè?'

'No. Too public. I'll come to your place.'

'Straight away?'

'No. They haven't finished the questioning yet. This is just a coffee break. I'll text you when I'm finally allowed to get away.' Then, with a touch of humour she didn't quite believe in, she added, 'That is, assuming I'm allowed to get away.'

I knew I should have gone back to try and sort out Ashleigh's problems, but I couldn't focus on them. I went home, as tense as a teenager whose on-off boyfriend has promised he'll call.

I couldn't settle to anything. Mindless activity was required, so I did some housework. I sometimes think, if it weren't for the necessity of sometimes shutting out unwelcome thoughts, my house would never get cleaned.

Even if I hadn't had Ben's Full English, I wouldn't have stopped for lunch. I was too wound up.

It was after three thirty when Hilary rang to say she was on her way. She's normally very good at keeping her emotions under control, but her voice sounded tight.

I couldn't even concentrate on housework until she arrived. I offered her coffee or 'something stronger'. She chose coffee. I knew her tastes and she followed me through into the kitchen while I made it. A decent coffeemaker is one of the luxuries I think I deserve.

'Listen, Ellen,' she said, 'we've both spoken to Prendergast now.'

'Yes.'

'So, I think it's important that we coordinate our stories.'

'OK,' I agreed cautiously.

'Obviously, we've both been a bit Jesuitical about what we've told him.'

'What do you mean by that?'

'Everything we've told him is true, but we have not necessarily told him all of the truth. So, we need to agree which bits of the truth we've left out – and which bits of the truth we intend to keep leaving out.'

'Give me some examples,' I said, handing across her flat white.

'From what Prendergast said to me, you'd mentioned my research with the lifers at Gradewell.'

'I could hardly have avoided that, could I? Anyway, that's information he could have got from any number of sources. From the governor of Gradewell, for a start.'

'I'm not questioning that. But you didn't mention to Prendergast that I knew Nate Ogden was likely to have gone to ground at Walnut Farm.'

'I didn't know that for a fact. I might have assumed it, but you hadn't told me in so many words. I told him that you'd agreed to meet me at Walnut Farm, but I didn't mention the connection with Nate Ogden.'

'Good. Incidentally, they told me the time you got there. Why did you arrive late?'

I realized I hadn't told her about the overnight crisis with my son. 'Suddenly had to sort something out with Ben,' I said.

Hilary did know a bit about his mental health problems, but she'd never talk about it if I hadn't raised the subject. Another of the ground rules in our relationship.

'You did go there, though?' I asked. 'To Walnut Farm.'

'Yes. I waited for you for half an hour, and then went back to Wittering.'

'And did you find Nate Ogden's body? Before I did?'

'No. There was no sign of him there.'

'So, he must've died between the time you left . . . which was, what . . . ?'

'Seven fifteen? Round then.'

'And the time I arrived with Ben, which was . . . probably quarter to ten.'

'Yes. Giving him a full hour and a half to top himself.'

For a nanosecond I was about to tell her that Nate Ogden didn't 'top himself', that he had in fact been murdered, but some instinct prevented me. I can be Jesuitical too when required. All truth, but not necessarily all of the truth.

'Presumably, Hilary, Prendergast didn't tell you that he suspected Nate of Kerry Tallis's murder?'

'No. But he did go as far as suggesting the two incidents might be linked.'

'Which we could have worked out from the fact that he's in charge of both investigations.'

'I suppose so.'

'What do you think happened, Hilary?'

'With Nate?

'Mm.'

Hilary did one of her pauses, collecting her thoughts. 'I think he probably did kill Kerry – and then topped himself out of guilt – or, more likely, because he knew the police were bound to catch up with him. I can understand why Nate went to his mother's house. What I can't get is why Kerry Tallis went there.'

'Oh, I may be able to help you then.' No reason not to pass on to her what I'd learned from Les about Maureen Ogden's prize draw win – and the likelihood that she'd kept the proceeds in a shoebox under her bed. Which information might just have been too alluring for someone with a heroin habit like Kerry's. Then, if Nate Ogden had surprised her stealing from the house of his recently deceased mother . . .

'You *have* been doing your research,' said Hilary, in a manner that wasn't entirely complimentary.

'I'm just intrigued by the whole thing. Also looking to protect myself.'

'How do you mean?'

'In the last few days, I've been the person to discover the bodies of two people dead in suspicious circumstances. Inevitably, the police are going to be questioning me further. Self-preservation dictates that one of the ways I can get them off my back is by finding out how Kerry Tallis and Nate Ogden actually died.'

'Becoming an amateur sleuth?'

'Of necessity. More coffee? I could do with another.'

'Please.'

As I busied myself with the machine, I said, 'Interesting to meet Liam on Sunday . . .'

'Oh yes,' she said vaguely. He was clearly way down her current list of priorities.

'Did he just stay at the cottage that night?'

'No, he's been there since.'

I shook my head in exasperation. 'You do make trouble for yourself, Hilary.'

'What do you mean?'

'Haven't you noticed that Liam's obsessed with you?'

'Oh, don't be ridiculous. I'm old enough to be his mother.'

'And don't you realize how attractive an older woman can be to someone of his age?'

'You're talking nonsense.'

'So, you've left him at the cottage?'

'I'm not sure.'

'What on earth do you mean by that?'

'He was certainly there before Prendergast and his sidekick arrived, because I talked to him through his bedroom door. When I left to come here, I shouted out, but there was no response.'

'Oh? Let's take our coffee through.'

When we'd sat down again, I asked the direct question. 'Are you all right, Hilary?'

'Not you too.'

'What do you mean?'

'I talked to Philip just before I came here. He asked exactly the same question.' So, he too had noticed the hairline cracks in her customary self-possession.

'He was worried because you weren't answering your phone.'

'Look, all that's happened is that I've spent a morning being questioned by the police. Not a very pleasant experience, in anyone's book. But I'm *all right*!' The vehemence with which she said the words undermined their meaning. 'And now,' she went on, 'Philip's insisting on coming down to the cottage to "support me", as he put it.'

'Philip's coming down here? On a weekday?'

'Yes, he's insisting.' Hilary looked at her watch. 'He'll be driving down now.'

What she said made me realize how little I actually knew about Philip and Hilary's marriage. The self-sufficiency they both showed to the outside world was maybe not as strong as it appeared. Contrary to appearances, Philip was aware of an inner fragility in his wife. A shortcoming which, even given our closeness as friends, she had never shared with me. This revelation of weakness increased my fondness for her.

But I didn't make any comment. The distinguished surgeon Philip Boredean was abandoning his day's work to 'support' his wife. That was all I needed to know.

'Anyway,' I said, 'back to Detective Inspector Prendergast . . . which particular part of your recent activities do you want to keep secret from him?'

'Sorry?'

'Which bits of the truth do you intend to keep leaving out?'

'Ah. With you. Right, I haven't told him that I went to Walnut Farm yesterday evening.'

'Why ever not?'

'Because I thought it would sound unprofessional.'

'Unprofessional in what way?'

'Unprofessional as regards my work as an academic. I'm doing this PhD on lifers. That means I can interview them, delve into their psyches, but it doesn't mean I can help them to evade justice.'

I saw what she meant. Knowing the hideout Nate Ogden was likely to use but keeping that information from the authorities at Gradewell and the police . . . yes, that could come under the heading of 'unprofessional'. Not to mention 'perverting the course of justice'.

'So, Ellen, if you can keep that from Prendergast . . .?'

'Sorry, too late.'

'You mean you've already told him?'

'Of course I have. He asked me the direct question. As he was bound to do. What reason would I have had for going to Walnut Farm if you hadn't suggested meeting me there?'

I was struck by an anomaly. I had told Prendergast the previous evening that Hilary had fixed to meet me at Walnut Farm. She had told him this morning she hadn't gone there. He must've spotted the inconsistency, and yet he didn't question her about it. Which made me think that the inspector was perhaps following some devious plan of his own. I should be on my guard.

Hilary's beautiful face looked crestfallen. What she'd asked was typical of her, though, I thought. Always having higher standards for herself, never wanting to be shown up. Desperate not to threaten her credentials as an academic.

But still vulnerable enough for her workaholic husband to put supporting her above the demands of his surgery.

Dodge brought Ben back about five thirty. He was on his way to lead a session at ReProgramme. It was clear that, for both of them, the day had been a success. Dodge had been glad of help with the heavy lifting, and Ben had become intrigued with the ingenuity of the recycling on display. He'd even volunteered his painting skills to decorate some of the artefacts, and Dodge had not ruled out the idea.

I realized something I should have realized long before, that Dodge was the perfect companion for my son. His own experiences had brought him great empathy with human suffering. Of course, he'd undergone some relevant training at ReProgramme. And the work he was willing to share with Ben was purely physical. The best kind of therapy for an unsettled mind. A bit like housework was for me.

I knew I mustn't take advantage of his good nature, but I recognized that Dodge could prove a useful occasional resource in dealing with my son.

After the Tipper had driven away, I could tell that Ben was still in a heightened mood, though not so manic as he had been the day before.

'I'll cook this evening,' I said. 'After that Full English you produced this morning. One of my lasagnes OK?'

'Fabulous, Ma. Dodge did produce cheese sandwiches at lunch-time, but I feel pretty peckish now.'

Over dinner, I was encouraged to hear that during the day Ben had rung a friend from Nottingham. 'Decided I've been having too much of my own company. Not, obviously, that I'm denigrating having *your* company, Ma.'

I grinned. 'No offence taken.'

'Anyway, I've fixed to meet her up in London tomorrow.'

'Her' was promising. As I mentioned, because of his mental condition, Ben's relationship history has been somewhat fractured. I'm not only speaking as a proud mum when I say that he's very attractive, and when he's in full flow in one of his more manic moods, he can be a mesmerizing talker. He has no problem in attracting female interest.

In this, of course, he's just like his father. And just like his father's, his moods shift. So Ben could leave a party with the telephone number of a girl who'd been spellbound by him all evening and wake up the next morning in such a state of self-loathing that he'd never get round to ringing her. Their closeness of the night before, his mind told him, had been just a flash in the pan. He wasn't worthy of her. They had no future. He'd only mess up her life.

In this, he was again just like Oliver. It was only after we'd been together for a while on the houseboat that Oliver had told me how nearly he hadn't rung me after our first, post-Waterstone's snowy encounter. What had seemed so simple in the pub that evening had become enormously complicated the following morning. Thoughts of the age difference, his glibness, his general unworthiness had, in his mind, made it almost impossible for him to dial my number.

What I had put down to his cavalier insouciance in not ringing me had been something much more complex.

I still thank God daily that my attraction for him beat off the negative thoughts.

So, the casual mention of my son going to meet a girl was music to my ears. Far too canny a mother, though, to ask any follow-up questions, I poured glasses of Merlot for both of us, and waited to see if Ben would volunteer further information.

I had to wait a while, as I often do, but over the lasagne he told me that her name was Tracey, that she wasn't at Nottingham Trent, she was at the older established University of Nottingham. They had met at a rock concert.

'What's she reading?' I dared to ask.

'Criminology.'

'Oh, so she's a postgraduate?' With my question came a mother's instinctive calculation: older than him then.

'No,' said Ben. 'It's her first degree. She's in her second year.'

I stopped myself from saying that I knew the University of Nottingham only did postgraduate degrees in criminology. Because I remembered where I had got that information from.

And I wondered why Liam Burgess would have lied about something like that.

# NINETEEN

I slept better that night – thank God – and woke up determined to pay more meaningful visits to Queenie and Ashleigh. I felt guilt for my lack of focus the day before. I must make it up to them and, hopefully, ease the tension between Ashleigh and her neighbours

Ben was already up, dressed, breakfasted and ready to cycle to Chichester Station before I made it to the kitchen. The British Museum was running an exhibition on the history of printing which he'd talked of visiting, and here was his perfect opportunity.

'What, so you'll go and see it before you meet Tracey for lunch?'

My son blushed. 'Actually, we're going to meet at the museum. She's interested in that stuff too.'

This suggestion that the two of them knew each other quite well was, of course, exactly what a mother wanted to hear. It was wonderful to see Ben so positive.

'Well, have a great time.'

'I will,' he said, as he moved to the front door.

'And . . .'

'I'm fine, Ma.'

Not sure when I would eat next, I made myself a mushroom omelette. I was just about to start on it when the phone rang.

'Hello. It's Bruce Tallis.'

'Ah. I do want to say how sorry I am for your loss. I don't know how—'

'All right, don't bother with all that. I know what you mean.' He moved brusquely on. 'I hear from the police you were the person who actually found her . . . Kerry's . . .' Somehow he couldn't say the word 'body' or 'corpse'.

'Yes, I did,' I said, trying to ease the awkwardness.

'They told me it was coincidence, that it happened to be you, someone who'd met Kerry before.'

'Yes, it was,' I confirmed.

'Was it *really*?' he asked.

'Of course it was. Are you suggesting I had anything to do with her death?'

'No, no, no,' he backtracked quickly. 'It's just that . . . I'm desperate to find out anything about her . . . her last days. Who she was hanging out with, how she came to end up in that flat . . . anything, really.'

'I'm afraid I'd seen nothing of your daughter between the end of our . . . business dealings . . .' The memory still brought an unpleasant taste to my mouth '. . . and when I discovered her body.'

'I was afraid you'd say that.' His voice took on an almost pathetic, pleading tone. 'But do you know anyone else who saw her, you know, during the last months?'

Of course, there was Les. Les, who'd spent time with 'Celeste' when they'd both crashed back into using after meeting at ReProgramme. But I wasn't about to land Les with his girlfriend's grieving father. Not until I'd checked it was OK with him, anyway.

'No,' I said. 'I can't think of anyone.'

'Listen, Ellen, I feel rather bad about you.'

'Oh?'

'The way I treated you way back.' He wasn't finding this easy. His previous career hadn't trained him in the skills of pleading and apologizing. 'I believed Kerry when she said you'd helped yourself to the proceeds from the stuff that my wife . . . you know what I mean.'

I did, but I saw no reason to make things easy for him.

He continued, more awkwardly than ever. 'The fact is, I now think Kerry may have taken the money herself.'

I still said nothing.

'So . . . I'll pay you what was on your invoice. Double what was on your invoice.' For men like Bruce Tallis, the solution to every problem was the application of more money.

But no amount of money could bring his daughter back to life. I thanked him formally for the offer of settlement. Then, after a silence, he said, 'I'd really like to meet up and talk about Kerry.'

'It wouldn't be a very long conversation,' I said. 'I hardly knew her, and you know the circumstances of our meeting.'

'Please.' His mouth had difficulty in shaping the unfamiliar word.

I thought about it. Here was me trying to find out the circumstances of Kerry Tallis's death, and here was her father, who had known her right through her life, offering the opportunity to talk about her. It was a no-brainer. I agreed to talk to him. Queenie and Ashleigh would once again be elbowed by a stronger priority.

I gave him my address and he said he'd drive straight down from Lorimers.

I was surprised that Les answered on the third ring.

He sounded disappointed when I identified myself. 'Oh, I thought it might be Dodge. He said he was going to ring this morning.'

I thought that was promising news – it suggested that Les might be rehabilitated into the ReProgramme community – but I made no comment. Instead I just told him about my recent conversation and Bruce Tallis's eagerness to talk to anyone who'd had recent contact with his daughter.

Les sounded dubious. 'I don't know. I've done my bit with the police, answered all their questions about Celeste, and finally got them off my back. Last thing I want to do is stir things up again.'

'I can see that. Well, fine. I won't put Bruce in touch with you.'

'Right.' He havered for a moment. 'Mind you, there are things I'd like to ask him about her. My relationship with Celeste was never going anywhere, relationships between people like us never do go anywhere, but I did care for her, you know.'

'I could easily give Bruce Tallis your number.'

'Mm.' He didn't sound keen. 'What's he look like, this Bruce Tallis?'

'Late fifties, early sixties, I suppose. Why're you asking?'

'Just, living the life I lead, you get very careful about people who're interested in meeting you. Never know who they are. Could be undercover cops, heavies come to get you for some drug deal that went wrong. You get a bit paranoid, you know. I'm not going to set up a meeting with someone who might be about to do me in.'

'Bruce Tallis only wants to talk to you about his daughter.'

'Oh yes? And suppose he's got it into his head that, because I was one of the last people to spend time with her, I was the one who topped her?'

'Now you *are* being paranoid.'

'Yeah? With reason. You'd understand that, if you'd lived through some of the things I have.'

I sighed. 'All right then. I won't give Bruce your number. But if you do want to know what he looks like, check out whether you do know him, I'm sure there are images online. He's quite a well-known figure in the business world.' I gave Les the details of Bruce Tallis's company.

'I might have a look,' he said. But not in the manner of someone who was about to do anything.

# TWENTY

As I ended the call, I saw through the front window a Jaguar SUV drawing up in front. Bruce Tallis was in the passenger seat, dressed in a suit and tie, perhaps on the way to the office, and driven by his butler/factotum Ramiro. It struck me this was the perfect opportunity to take a photograph I could send to Les. If he didn't recognize Bruce as a potential danger, then perhaps he might be prepared to talk to him.

I took the photo through the window and opened the front door. I invited Ramiro to come in, but Bruce said he would stay in the car. The Portuguese did not raise any objection, giving the impression that he was well used to waiting around at his employer's pleasure. There didn't seem to be much warmth between the two men, but then this was the first time I'd seen them together, so perhaps it reflected a permanent state of affairs.

'Ramiro will not be with me much longer,' Bruce volunteered as he came into the house. 'He is going back to Albufeira to open a restaurant. I cannot think he will make a success of it. He's a lazy bastard, doesn't understand the meaning of hard work.'

I remembered hearing Constancia's similar view, that if their restaurant ever did get opened, it was she who would end up doing everything.

'Anyway, first thing I must do . . .' Bruce reached into his inside pocket and produced an envelope. 'What I owe you,' he said brusquely. 'Doubled up.' Money once again solving everything?

He did not react to my thanks and refused the offer of coffee or tea. He said, 'I'm just here because I want to talk about Kerry. Her mother – you know, my first wife – won't have anything to do with me. And my second wife . . .' Once again, he avoided using her name.

'Jeanette,' I said firmly.

'Yes. Well, she never really knew Kerry, so . . . there are very few people I can talk to about her. That's why I've come to you.'

His reasoning seemed slightly odd, but I suppose one doesn't expect too much logic from someone who's just suffered a devastating bereavement. So, with the warning that I probably couldn't provide much new information, I said he could ask any questions he wished to. I'd made myself a coffee and we sat in the sitting room.

'Needless to say,' he began, 'I've had a lot of interviews with the police since . . . since, er . . .'

'Detective Inspector Prendergast?'

'Him and others, yes. They're still very curious about why you ended up in that flat, you know, where you found Kerry . . .'

'Are they?'

'Yes. I think Prendergast's probably going to want to talk to you a lot more.'

'He implied as much to me.'

'I just thought you should know that, you know, from what he said to me.'

'Fine. I'll be ready for him.'

'I wonder, Ellen, if you could go through, for me, the precise circumstances of how you found my daughter . . . my daughter's . . .'

I had no wish to repeat the narrative yet again, but I reasoned that his bereavement deserved that much effort from me, however unwelcome. As we talked, he gave me insights into where Kerry had gone wrong in life. He laid much of the blame on her mother, ignoring his own long absences and lack of parental input. He didn't know exactly when Kerry had started using heroin, but he thought it was in her late teens. And he issued wild threats about what he would do if he ever tracked down the people who had introduced her to the drug and continued to supply it to her.

For a long time he hadn't realized, as his beloved daughter asked for ever greater increases in her allowance, what she was spending the money on. When he did, he cut back sharply on the subsidies. But rather than breaking her habit, that had only made her turn to crime to fund it.

'Crime like taking the money for the returns on Jeanette's purchases?' I suggested. 'And blaming it on me?'

'Yes,' he said unwillingly.

'And stealing from your golf club friends?'

That really shocked him. 'How did you hear about that?'

No way I was going to involve Dodge, so I just said, 'One hears things.'

'Well, for God's sake, don't mention it to anyone else!' His membership of the West Sussex seemed more important to him than his recent tragedy.

He asked me more questions about my discovery of Kerry's corpse. He was so insistent, constantly going over the same ground, how I came to be in Portsmouth and so on, that for a while I wondered whether he suspected me of being responsible for his daughter's death.

But, as our conversation drew to a close, that impression was replaced by another one. Bruce Tallis did not suspect me of murder; he was just trying to find out how much I knew. Whether I had any information that might lead to identifying the real perpetrator.

A cynic, who suspected Bruce Tallis's guilt in the case, might have thought that he was checking whether he had covered his tracks adequately.

After he'd left, I texted the photograph I had taken of Bruce Tallis to Les. I had this nice fantasy that he'd get back to me straight away, saying whether or not he recognized the man. But he didn't reply and, as I told myself discouragingly, there was no reason why he ever should.

I tried to appease my conscience by visiting Queenie and Ashleigh, but again my concentration was bad. I did at least ensure that Queenie ate another Hobnob, but I hadn't got the energy to be proactive on Ashleigh's case. And, increasingly, if she was going to keep her flat and keep Zak out of care, she needed someone to be proactive.

So, I got back home in a state of dissatisfaction. I tried to do more housework, but that didn't engage me. My mind was too full of Kerry Tallis.

Could it really be that Bruce had killed his own daughter? What was that line Oliver was always quoting to me? Oscar Wilde, I think. 'Yet each man kills the thing he loves.' Surely it wasn't possible.

I settled down to organize my recent SpaceWoman invoices

into a form in which they could be sent to my accountant for the tax return. That was almost as mindless as housework, but it didn't stop my thoughts from straying as much as I would have wished.

I'd had a text from Ben late afternoon to say when he'd be back. He's good like that, particularly after he's had one of his 'incidents'. I contemplated the further displacement activity of cooking a lavish dinner for him. I can get quite pleasantly involved in cooking when the mood takes me. But then I recalled that I didn't know what scale of lunch he'd have had in London with Tracey. Better wait till he came home and see how hungry he was.

I tried the television, but the daytime schedule is such mindless dross that it didn't engage me. And I knew I hadn't got the concentration to embark on some meaty drama from Netflix. I poured myself a glass of Merlot at five o'clock, much earlier than I normally would have done, then went and had a long bath with a second one.

As he had promised, Ben arrived back soon after seven and I could tell as soon as he came through the door that the day had been a good one. He and Tracey had got on. When I asked about his lunch, I was glad I hadn't gone to the effort of cooking something elaborate for the evening. He said they hadn't left the restaurant until after four. Which I thought was very good news.

I didn't ask him anything about Tracey. I didn't want to be a mother in the Fleur Bonnier mould, eager to squeeze out every last detail about her child's sex life (though in her case to demonstrate how inadequate it was as compared to her own). But the few details Ben did let slip warmed my maternal heart.

I wondered whether Tracey had had anything to do with his recent low mood. He had always found sustaining relationships difficult and, at his lowest, was as sensitive as if he'd had layers of skin removed. But, anyway, if there had been a problem between them, the day seemed to have resolved it.

'One interesting thing Tracey did, Ma . . .'

'Oh yes?' I tried not to sound too pathetically interested in any information he was volunteering about her.

'You remember you were talking about that guy Liam Burgess . . . the one who's been working with Hilary . . .?'

'Mm.'

'Well, as you know, Tracey's not at Nottingham Trent, she's at the University of Nottingham.'

'Yes.'

'Doing a BA in criminology. And you said Liam was doing a postgraduate degree in the same subject.'

'Hm?'

'Well, she'd never met him.'

'Is that strange? I mean, I've no idea exactly how many students there might be doing criminology in—'

'Tracey checked on her laptop while we were having lunch. She obviously has access to all the university records.'

'Does she?'

'Yes. And the interesting thing she found out was—'

'Stop being overdramatic, Ben. Tell me.'

'There's nobody called Liam Burgess registered at the University of Nottingham. Undergraduate or postgraduate.'

# TWENTY-ONE

I didn't sleep so well that night. No choking dreams, just restless. I woke at 2.43. Isn't it annoying how precise digital clocks have made us? When I was younger, I could wake 'round quarter to three'. Not any more. As soon as I wake, the LED numbers are imprinted on my brain.

That night, with consciousness came a bleak feeling of missing Oliver. It still happens distressingly often. I suppose that's something that'll be with me for the rest of my life.

I tried to replace thoughts of him with work issues. During the previous week – amazing, it was still less than a week – I'd had to postpone some bookings. First thing in the morning I must reschedule them. And chase the invoices which my brief investigations of the day before had revealed to be unpaid.

I did go back to sleep eventually. And then woke round the time I normally do: 6.37. Precise again. Friday morning.

Ben and I had had a very pleasant evening together, but he hadn't said what his plans were. Though he'd clearly enjoyed his time with Tracey, I was still worried about him. Didn't want him to be alone all day. And I couldn't call on Dodge again so soon. Whereas I might have made my necessary SpaceWoman phone calls from the Yeti on my rounds, I decided to do them from home until I'd found out what Ben was intending to do.

But plans were abruptly changed by my phone ringing soon after seven. Philip Boredean.

'Can you come over here, Ellen?'

'What's happened?'

'Hilary. She's disappeared.'

'What?'

'I came down yesterday late afternoon. There was no sign of her. I haven't slept all night, thinking where she might be.'

'I'm sure she can't have gone far. I saw her only a couple of days ago. She came over here. She was fine.'

'Well, I don't think she's fine now.'

I was worried. Philip's not the kind of man to get hysterical. He's very even-tempered – almost, I've realized over the years, to the point of being dull. That was why I was so glad I'd not ended up with him. Life with Oliver had been a roller-coaster, at times very scary, but it had never been dull.

But for Philip to ring, in the kind of state he clearly was, worried me.

'Do you know something? There was no note, was there? Are you afraid she's been kidnapped or . . .?'

'No, not that. I'm afraid . . . I'm afraid . . .'

'What are you afraid of, Philip?'

There was a silence. Then he said, 'Liam's disappeared too.'

'Yes. Hilary said there was no sign of him when she left the house on Wednesday.'

'But I've looked in the room he was sleeping in. He left his laptop. I'm sure there's stuff on it that . . . I couldn't access it, but . . .'

I repeated, 'What are you afraid of, Philip?'

The answer, when it came, was like a cry of anguish. 'I'm afraid Hilary's gone off with Liam.'

And I realized I didn't know as much as I thought I did about my friends' marriage.


If accessing data on a laptop was going to be required, I needed someone with me who knew about computers. He wasn't aware of it yet, but I had sorted out how Ben was going to spend his day.

I woke him up and told him what was happening. While he was dressing, I made him a bacon sandwich (heavy on the ketchup, just as he likes it) to eat in the car. Then we set off in the Yeti for West Wittering.

I had never before seen Philip in the state he was in. I had never before realized how utterly dependent he was on Hilary. You wouldn't have guessed it from his customary laid-back attitude, his obsession with his work.

'No sign of her?' I asked.

He shook his head.

'Or of Liam?'

'No.'

It wasn't appropriate for me to get Ben involved in Philip's fears of his wife's infidelity, so I said, 'You mentioned stuff on his laptop . . .?'

'Yes.'

'Perhaps, if you're happy for him to do so, Ben could take a look at that while we chat?'

'Good idea.' Philip gave an elaborate throat-clearing, as if that would shake him out of his vulnerability. 'Come upstairs and I'll show you.'

The spare room was as immaculately appointed as everything else in the cottage, but not as tidy. The duvet was half on the floor, there were clothes scattered over the chairs. And the window opened out on to the roof of the conservatory beneath.

'Looks like that's how he made his exit,' I suggested. 'And in a hurry.'

'A real hurry, to leave his laptop behind,' Ben contributed. He knew how essential a bit of kit that was to any student.

'Possibly,' said Philip.

'If you're happy for Ben to have a look . . .?'

'Sure, sure. I tried, but it kept asking for passwords.'

'I might be able to get round that,' said Ben, confident of his generation's techie know-how.

Philip lingered, uncharacteristically inert. I'd never seen him not being proactive.

'Why don't we go down and have a coffee,' I suggested gently. 'You want one, Ben love?'

'I'm fine, Ma.'

The conservatory didn't get the morning sun. Philip and I sat opposite each other, coffees on a low table between us.

I put the straight question. 'Do you honestly think that Hilary's run off with Liam?'

'What else is there to think?'

I could have come up with a great many answers to that, but it wasn't the moment. 'Has she said anything to you about him?'

'No, but . . . well, she wouldn't in the circumstances, would she?'

'Look, you know over the years she has worked with quite a lot of younger men?'

'Yes.'

'And, well, frankly because she's so bloody beautiful, a lot of them have fallen for her.'

'I know that.'

'And didn't that worry you?'

'God, no. It amused me. It amused us. We used to giggle about it.'

That suggested a level of light-heartedness in their marriage which I wouldn't have suspected. But was encouraged to hear about.

'So Hilary was aware of the effect she had on these young men?'

'Of course she was. She liked it. I think it gave her extra validation, as a woman. I liked it too. It was as if I had actually won the prize that so many men lusted after. Our marriage was strong, and that was all that mattered to me.'

'So why is Liam different? Why are you worried about him if you weren't worried about the others?'

'Because Hilary's changed in the last few months.'

'Oh?'

'Well, as you know, she's always had a high level of insecurity . . .'

That came as something of a bombshell to me. No, I hadn't known that. Of all the women I knew, I would have said Hilary was the most confident. She had a high level of expectation for herself, yes, but not insecurity. Though, when I came to think about it, the two could be opposite sides of the same coin. I felt chastened for my ignorance of my best friend's real personality.

But all I said to Philip was, 'Yes.'

'I mean, some elements of it have always been there. You know, having had the father she did.'

'She never talked to me about her father.'

'Didn't she? Really?'

'No.'

'Hilary's father was Gerry Cruden.'

'Gerry Cruden the journalist?'

'Yes.'

He must have died at least ten years ago, but Gerry Cruden was a name that had been hard to escape for a couple of decades before that. He was a right-wing controversialist who worked for a lot of national newspapers in the old days of Fleet Street, and then found a permanent soapbox as a columnist for the *Daily Mail*. If he was as much of a bully in his private life as he was on the printed page, then it was no surprise that Hilary had described her childhood as 'private grief'.

'I had no idea.'

'It wasn't something she advertised. She wouldn't have told me, except there was some life insurance paperwork we had to sort out for which I needed the details of her parents. Of course, I never met him, which I gather was a blessing. Very hard man to please, from all accounts. Nothing Hilary could do was ever good enough for him.'

A few other details clicked into place. Hilary's desperate need to succeed, to prove herself. Maybe the creative writing courses had been attempts to beat her father at his own game . . .?

But while I was still processing one bombshell, Philip detonated another. 'And then, of course, there's Hilary's sense of inferiority in relation to you . . .'

I couldn't stop myself from uttering an incredulous: 'What?'

'Things have got much worse in the last year, though. I don't know if it's her age . . .' I'm always amused by the lengths men will go to to avoid using the word 'menopause' '. . . but she's become very . . . I'm not sure what the right word is. "Paranoid", perhaps? She really worries about losing her looks. I suppose age is cruel to someone as beautiful as she is.'

Something I've never had to worry about, I thought, still reeling from the thought that Hilary might be jealous of me.

'Anyway, I was thinking . . .' Philip went on, 'I mean, I've seen enough movies about this kind of thing . . . that a woman worried about her fading charms might be susceptible to adoration from a younger man.'

'Like Liam, are you suggesting?'

'Yes, I suppose I am.'

'Well, you know Hilary better than I do.' A lot better, I was beginning to realize. 'But I would be very surprised if that's what's happened. I think it's much more likely her disappearance has something to do with events at Walnut Farm.'

'Walnut Farm?'

'The place where the body of Nate Ogden, the lifer Hilary had been working with, was discovered.'

'What?' Panic lit his normally placid eyes. 'You mean she's involved with criminals? That they might have abducted her?'

'No, no,' I soothed. 'Look, you know Nate Ogden is believed to have murdered the girl whose body I found in the flat in Portsmouth?'

'I'd heard that, yes.'

'I've been trying to find out the truth of what happened there. In both cases, actually. Partly, that's to get the police off my back.'

'Are they on your back?'

'They will be. I'm sure they haven't finished with me yet. By unlucky coincidence, I was the first person to discover both bodies. So far as the police are concerned, that makes me a very suspicious person. Only finding out who actually committed the murders will get me off the hook.'

'Murders in the plural? I thought the convict topped himself.'

'Yes, of course, sorry. I was getting mixed up.' Forgetting who was meant to know what.

'What's this got to do with Hilary's disappearance?'

'Well, if I know Hilary . . .' Though now I wondered whether I did '. . . she is at least as curious by nature as I am. And since she was involved in my appearing at both crime scenes, the police will have an unhealthy interest in her too. I would think what she is currently doing is her bit of amateur sleuthing, trying to find out the truth of what happened.'

'And that's meant to comfort me, is it? The idea that my wife has been away all night investigating a murder? I think I'd rather—'

What he'd rather I never found out, because at that moment the cottage shook and creaked as my son came thundering down the stairs and into the conservatory.

'I've got some rather interesting news,' he said. He was glowing with excitement.

'From Liam's laptop?'

'That's right, Ma. Except it isn't Liam's laptop.'

'What do you mean?'

'Liam Burgess does not exist.'

Philip and I went up to the spare room with Ben, who demonstrated what he had discovered. First, he told us a lot of technical detail about how he'd accessed the password-protected files. I didn't listen, it meant nothing to me.

It was then with considerable, and justifiable – come on, I am his mother – pride that Ben revealed the real name of the laptop's owner. Ricky Brewer.

Philip was less than impressed. 'Liam might just have stolen the laptop from someone of that name.'

'No,' said Ben firmly. 'I've managed to access his emails. In some he definitely says he's using the alias of "Liam Burgess".'

'Are there any sent to Hilary?' asked Philip with sudden urgency.

'Have a look.' Ben opened the relevant window.

I saw no reason not to peer over Philip's shoulder. It didn't feel like intruding on his privacy. There were four emails from 'Liam' to Hilary. All had attached academic papers about the psychology of prisoners sentenced to life, research which she must have asked him to dig out. In none of them were any personal sentiments expressed. There was no mention of love.

Having found that out, Philip lost interest. He went downstairs to phone around some of their friends and see if Hilary had been in touch. He wasn't optimistic about the results, but he didn't want to report her as a missing person yet.

I stayed with Ben and the laptop. The news of Liam's false identity had set a whole new cavalcade of logic racing in my mind.

First, I got Ben to go back to the computer and find out anything he could about Ricky Brewer. There was surprisingly little. The laptop was new and the email account had only been opened a few weeks earlier. Maybe Ricky Brewer – if it was him – had bought it for one specific project and not imported any personal data from his previous machine.

Though it couldn't help me with details about its owner, it was still a working laptop, offering all kinds of online information. My mind was working very quickly and clearly now. I knew what the next step had to be.

Ben's interest in fonts meant that he had access to the archives of a lot of newspapers. There's so much of that stuff online these days. I knew what I was looking for and, under my direction, he very quickly found what I had hoped he would find.

Yesss!

# TWENTY-TWO

In my call to Dorothy Lechlade, I said I was just checking she was in. I imagine she thought I was making contact about the prospective decluttering of her husband's workspace.

I dropped Ben at home – there was some comedy stuff he wanted to catch up with on Netflix – and printed up the research he'd found for me. I put it in a folder. I thought Ben'd be all right for a couple of hours on his own. He was really energized by his success with the laptop at the cottage. I hoped he'd ring Tracey to tell her about it.

Philip had had no objection to my taking the laptop from the cottage. I put it in the car, along with the folder.

I parked the Yeti directly outside Clovelly. I didn't care if the neighbours knew the Lechlades were having dealings with a declutterer.

The door was opened by Tobias, looking as charm-free as ever. His roguish smile was already in place; he knew it was me who was arriving. 'Can't keep away from me, eh?' he said.

'I've actually come to visit your wife,' I said.

'What's hers is mine.' He grinned. 'That's what marriage is about.'

He backed away to let me in, but not far enough. I had to pass too close to him to get into the hall. Once again, he smelled unwholesomely of tobacco. Dorothy emerged and ushered me into the sitting room. Now I knew why her face had looked familiar.

She offered me coffee and went through to the kitchen to make it, presumably with the old Cona percolator. The sitting room, like the rest of the house, had probably not been decorated for thirty years. Dorothy, I could see, was going to have an uphill struggle erasing her deceased in-laws' legacy.

Tobias sat on a sofa and patted the space beside him. I moved deliberately to plonk myself in an armchair. 'Listen,' I said, 'I want to talk to Dorothy on her own.'

'Oh, Dotty and I share—'

'I want to speak to her on my own,' I continued. 'And if you don't leave the room, I will tell her about your putting your hand on my breasts during my last visit.'

'Oh, that wasn't anything.'

'No? Putting a hand on a woman's breasts isn't anything?'

'Just a bit of fun. Nothing to get aerated about.'

'Shall I describe what you did to me to your wife and see if she gets "aerated" about it?'

'Don't be childish. I'm sure you wouldn't go and—'

'Want to try me?' I demanded.

Nothing more was said until Dorothy returned with the coffee. 'I'll take mine up with me,' her husband grunted. 'Some work I've got to get on with.'

She looked a little puzzled as he abruptly left the room and we heard his footsteps clumping up the stairs.

Then Dorothy said, 'It's very fortunate that you've come. It's sort of made a decision for me.'

'Sorry?'

'Well, I'm still keen to get Tobias's workspace sorted, and he's been dragging his feet about it, but now you've actually arrived, we can sort out—'

'I haven't come here about the decluttering.'

'Oh?'

'I've come here to talk about your former career.'

'As a teacher?'

'No, as a social worker.'

She coloured. 'That was a very long time ago.'

'And you gave up the job in rather unusual circumstances, didn't you?'

'I was very young at the time and—'

I pulled out the printed sheets of the newspaper cuttings Ben had found for me. I indicated one of the headlines. 'THE LOST BOYS SCANDAL', it read. 'I vaguely remember reading something about it at the time, but I had no reason to associate the name of "Dorothy Lechlade" with "Dorothy Brunton".'

'I was cleared by the investigation.'

'Cleared of criminal charges. Not cleared of incompetence.'

'Ellen, that was a very unhappy period of my life.'

'I'm sure it was.'

'Nothing I'd done in my training had prepared me for being responsible for children in that kind of situation. I was brought up in a very cushioned, middle-class way – "privileged" you might say – and I had this idealistic view that I had something to give to society. I never realized quite what society was like, real society, real life. I was far too young to have been put in charge of fostering those children.'

'I'm sure you were. Listen, Dorothy, I'm not here to blame you, or criticize you. From what I've read of the case, you were treated very badly by your employers, given no support at all.'

'I was so desperate to succeed. It was my first job.'

'I understand. And I'm sure you were very trusting. It's a failing that often goes along with idealism.' One that I'd suffered from a few times myself. 'Those people seemed like suitable foster parents. You weren't to know that they'd falsified their paperwork.'

'I didn't. I should have checked. So many things I should have done back then.'

I was stirring up memories that had been quiescent for a long time. I didn't want to hurt the woman, I just wanted to get information out of her. So I softened my tone as I said, 'I'm not here to be judgemental about you, Dorothy. You made the kind of mistakes that could have been made by anyone of that age, if they weren't properly supervised. When the investigation came out, there was much more blame attached to your bosses than there was to you.'

'That's true,' she said, determined to snatch at any thread of self-justification.

'All I want from you is some information about one of the boys.'

'Boys?' she echoed vaguely.

'One of the boys who was allocated to unsuitable foster parents.'

'Oh.'

I took out another scan of a fifteen-year-old newspaper's front page. This time the headline read: 'JUDGE SENTENCES "BRUTAL" KILLER OF GIRLFRIEND'. It concerned the end of the murder trial of Nate Ogden. 'You remember this case, Dorothy?'

'Yes. It happened round the same time as the investigation into the fostering scandal was published. Brought it all back into the news again.'

'Megan Evans was the name of Nate Ogden's victim. And she had a son who had been taken into care some years before her death.'

'Yes,' Dorothy confirmed without intonation.

'He was one of the ones you were responsible for? One of the ones who ended up with the abusing foster parents?'

Another flat 'Yes.'

'Was his surname "Evans" at that point?'

'Yes. But it was thought to be a good idea to change it after his mother's murder.'

'And what was the boy's name changed to, Dorothy?'

'Richard Brewer.'

Ben had shown me how to access the data, and as soon as I got back to the Yeti, I looked at some of the other stuff he'd found on Ricky Brewer's laptop. Though the young man had only had the machine a short time, there was still information from his search history about how he'd found out where Nate Ogden was completing his sentence, about how he had targeted Hilary Boredean as someone who had contact with the prisoner.

And then there was the revenge stuff. The unhinged rantings about how his life had been destroyed by his mother's murder. The determination to kill her killer as soon as he finished his sentence.

I didn't know where Ricky Brewer – or Liam Burgess – was, but I had found out the identity of Nate Ogden's killer. When I passed over my findings to Detective Inspector Prendergast, I would be off the hook for at least one of the murders.

# TWENTY-THREE

nvestigating the other murder would have to wait. I had more personal priorities.

One obviously was Ben. I came home from Clovelly to find a note from him on the kitchen table. 'Back up to London. Meeting up with Tracey again. Be back some time tomorrow. And I'm all right, Ma. More than all right.'

I took his word for it. And I was really encouraged by the fact that he was going to stay overnight. Funny, when did the moment come for a mother to be more worried by a son *not* sleeping with women than she was by him sleeping with them?

So that was one of my personal priorities solved. The other was Hilary. Unlike Philip, I wasn't really worried about her. For some reason, I didn't share his fears of her having been abducted. And yet the way he'd been unmanned by the fear of her running off with the young man we then thought of as Liam Burgess suggested that all was not as serene as their marriage appeared on the outside. Maybe Hilary's refusal to respond to Philip's calls was a way of punishing him for some unknown shortcoming.

She wasn't taking calls from her husband. Maybe she might take one from me.

The phone rang and rang, which was encouraging. It meant she was well enough to keep it charged, rather than lying in a ditch somewhere with her head caved in.

The answering message clicked on. Not Hilary's voice, just a generic one. But that's what she always used.

'Hilary,' I said, 'if you want to talk, please call me.' That was enough. No point in adding more.

She rang back within five minutes.

'Are you all right?' was my first question.

'I'm not quite sure what that means, Ellen. I'm not ill.'

'No. But you realize Philip's been frantic about your disappearance.'

'Has he? I'm surprised he noticed.'

Was that just a reference to his workaholic character or something deeper? Not the moment to investigate. 'Hilary, if you want to meet up and talk, I'd be happy to come to wherever you are.'

There was a long silence. Then she said, 'Maybe that would be a good idea. Better face one's demons, eh?'

Which struck me as a very odd thing to say.

I was not surprised to find that Hilary had simply booked into a hotel for the night. More of a pub with rooms than a hotel, really. Lovely seaside setting near Pagham Harbour Local Nature Reserve. Popular on summer evenings for the spectacular sunsets. Quite pricey, but money was never a problem for Philip and Hilary.

We had coffee in the garden by the sea. The view good enough for a brochure. No one else there mid-morning. No one to eavesdrop. No one to inhibit any revelations that might be made.

'It's about Liam,' Hilary said.

Oh dear. Had I got it all wrong? Had Philip been right all along? Was I about to hear some confession of illicit passion with a younger man? But all I said was, 'What about Liam?'

'I was such a fool about him.' That too might have been heading in the same direction, but then she added, 'I should have seen through him, seen what he was after from the start.'

I didn't want to unload all I had found out about Liam – or Ricky Brewer – until Hilary had told me how much she knew.

'I was a fool,' she repeated. 'I welcomed him in, believed his stories about studying criminology. I thought here was someone I could actually do some good for.'

'He appeared very plausible,' I said, 'on the one occasion I met him.'

'Yes, but I should have seen through him,' she insisted. 'It's not the first time I've got carried away by doing my Lady Bountiful routine.'

This was more self-knowledge than I had expected from her. 'When did you find out he wasn't who he claimed to be?' I asked.

'Tuesday. The day he did a runner. When I think about it, I should have realized.'

'Realized what?'

'Why he did a runner.'

'Hm?'

'It was the arrival of the police that frightened him off. You remember – Prendergast and his sidekick arrived that morning to talk to me. I came to see you straight after. It was the police coming that frightened Liam off.'

That made sense, explained the disarray I'd seen in his bedroom at the West Wittering cottage. He must have thought the police were coming for him.

'But did you find out who he really was?'

Hilary nodded painfully. 'After I got back from seeing you, I found papers in his room, stuff about his plans to kill Nate as soon as he was released. And I realized just how much information I had given him.'

'About Walnut Farm?'

'Yes. I was so proud about my lifers PhD, and he seemed to admire what I was doing so much . . . I was very indiscreet. Now I look back on it, I realize just how easily he set me up. Playing to my vanity. I answered every question Liam asked me about Nate Ogden. I'd spent a lot of time interviewing him at Gradewell over the last year. I knew a lot. And Liam just siphoned all that information off.'

'Including the fact that Nate might lie low at Walnut Farm?'

'Yes. Nate'd mentioned the place to me at some point, during one of our interviews. There was some dispute between the brothers who'd inherited the place, so they could never agree about selling it and it just went to rack and ruin. Nate said if he ever got in trouble with the police again, there was a hideout he could use. It was kind of a joke. But he meant it. Apparently, he went and checked the place out, to see that it was still unoccupied, after one of his visits to his mother.'

'And you told Liam?'

As she nodded, Hilary looked as if she was in actual physical pain. 'So, by the end of Tuesday afternoon, I knew that Liam was about to go to Walnut Farm to kill Nate. And I did nothing.' Tears welled over her lower lids and ran down the perfect face.

I tried to reassure her. 'You couldn't have known for certain that was going to happen.'

'No? I still knew enough to tell the police about the possibility.

But I didn't. And do you know why? Because I cared too much about my PhD. I didn't want anything to threaten my completing that. And, as a result, I allowed Nate Ogden to be murdered.'

'When you say you "cared too much about your PhD", what do you mean exactly?'

'I mean I'd got a good story about Nate Ogden and I wanted to follow it through.'

'Hm?'

'A good bit of investigative journalism. I knew there was a book in it.'

'A True Crime book?'

'Yes.' The blue eyes sparkled with enthusiasm. 'A potential bestseller.'

'And a book whose chances of becoming a bestseller would become greatly enhanced by ending with a murder? Where the son of the victim waits throughout the perpetrator's long prison sentence till he can exact his revenge?'

'Yes.' She liked my response, reading it as if I shared her enthusiasm for the project. And I realized how little I actually knew her.

'So,' I said evenly, 'you would finally have produced a work of investigative journalism that your father would have been proud of?'

The sparkle in her eyes dulled. 'How do you know about my father?'

'Philip told me.'

'Did he? I told him he should never mention it to anyone. But of course, for Philip, different rules apply when you're involved.'

I ignored that. I wasn't sure what she meant, anyway. There was a silence. I tried to convince myself that she was overstating her guilt in the case, but I knew she wasn't, really. If she had warned the police what was about to happen at Walnut Farm, Nate Ogden might still be alive. Possibly facing false charges for murdering Kerry Tallis, but still alive.

I tried to find an excuse for her behaviour. 'But you did try to intervene, didn't you? Presumably that was why you went to Walnut Farm that evening? To try to stop Liam from committing the murder?'

'I didn't go to Walnut Farm that evening.'

'What? OK, I know you told Prendergast you didn't go, but you arranged to meet me there.'

'I didn't go.'

'Then why did you send me there?'

There was a long silence. Then Hilary said, 'This is difficult.'

'I'm sure it is, but for God's sake tell me what you mean!'

'It goes back a long way. To when I first met you, Ellen. And I realized I could never be like you.'

'You don't have to be like me. That's why we get on. Because we're different.'

'Not what I meant. I meant I could never be as good as you.'

'Good?'

'Naturally good. I'm not like that. There's too much evil in me.'

'Evil? You haven't got an evil bone in your body.'

'Oh, I have, Ellen. A whole skeleton of them.'

For a moment I wondered if she was having me on, playing some elaborate joke. But the expression on her face told me that wasn't the case. And I remembered what Philip had said about her inexplicable sense of inferiority where I was concerned.

'Ellen, I've always been jealous of you.'

'Jealous? Why?'

'Because you have everything so sorted.'

'Sorted?' I thought about my life – a husband who had killed himself, a depressive son, a distant daughter, a difficult mother. How could anyone imagine my life was *sorted*?

'And, of course,' she went on with difficulty, 'there's you and Philip.'

'Me and Philip?'

'Yes. You were his first girlfriend.'

'I know I was his first girlfriend, Hilary, but we're talking more than thirty years ago and—'

'He's never met anyone who's matched up to you.'

'Don't be ridiculous! Philip adores you.'

'He still doesn't think I match up to you. You don't deny that you slept together, do you?'

'No, of course I don't. But in retrospect, I think we've both realized the sex wasn't even that good.'

'You may have realized that. Philip hasn't.'

'Has he ever talked to you about it?'

'No, it's not the kind of thing he would talk about.'

'Then how do you know he thinks that?'

'I just *know*.'

I realized now what I was up against. It never for a moment occurred to me that what she thought was true, that Philip genuinely found all women a disappointment after a few inept fumbles in bed with me. But I could see how deeply Hilary believed it, how she had hoarded these feelings of inferiority over the years, and how they had grown uncontrollable.

I knew, from living with Oliver, how thoughts like that can never be unthought. Paranoia, resentment against a person (however unjustified), self-loathing . . . though, in more stable moods they can be laughed off, the logic they once dictated leaves a permanent mark on the memory. And when the depression or paranoia returns, they can all too readily return with it. Like replaying the same track of music.

There was one thing I still needed to know from Hilary. 'So why did you send me to Walnut Farm on Tuesday?' A memory came to me. 'And was it you who sent me there the first time? Last Friday, when I found no one there? Did you set that up?'

'Yes,' she said coolly.

'But why?'

She looked me straight in the eye and said, without vindictiveness but with something that she regarded as perfect logic, 'I wanted to cause trouble for you. I wanted to hurt you, Ellen.'

Before I left the pub garden, I did persuade Hilary to call Philip. They had a lot to sort out. But it was between them. Or, if input from a third person was required, that person should be a psychiatrist. I wasn't going to get involved.

As I drove slowly back home, I tried to come to terms with Hilary's bizarre revelations. I would have said she was my best friend. But it just goes to show how impossible it is to know anyone fully.

I hoped we'd stay in touch, but I wasn't sure whether she'd still be my best friend.

\* \* \*

When I got home, the first thing I did was to check that Ben wasn't in his room, that he actually had gone to London. He had, but my old habits of vigilance die hard.

To my surprise, I found that I was very hungry. So, since I knew I wouldn't be able to settle to anything, I indulged myself with a proper lunch. One of my regular standbys: Spanish eggs with chorizo and peppers. Lovely. And, as I continued to puzzle over what I had heard from Hilary, I had a couple of glasses of Merlot from the bottle Ben and I had opened the previous evening.

I then lay down on the bed and, unsurprisingly, given the wine and the tensions of the last week, I slept for more than two hours.

I woke with a feeling of completion. I'd come to the end of one sequence of events. I had no idea how the police investigation into Kerry's death was going, but at least we knew who had killed Nate. I texted Philip, suggesting he should contact the police about Liam's actions. It was, after all, from his cottage that the murderer had done a runner. I was sure the police would want further information from me at some point, but at that moment I didn't want to have anything to do with them.

What I did fancy, though, was an evening in front of the telly. I've always got a lot of medical dramas recorded. My guilty secret, perhaps. Not that I feel guilty about it. Nothing I like better than people in scrubs shouting orders at each other while they negotiate their complex love lives.

I had got to the point in the story where the grandson of the old man with terminal cancer had just been brought into the same hospital after a cycling accident, when my phone alerted me that I'd got a text.

From Les. It read: 'Thanks for the photograph. I do recognize the bloke. He was Celeste's new dealer.'

# TWENTY-FOUR

As I drove towards Lorimers, I realized how delusional my sense of completion had been. There was no way I could relax until I had resolved the Tallis family's part of the mystery.

And now I knew that Bruce Tallis had been supplying drugs to his daughter during the last weeks of her life, I also knew that I had to confront him.

I brought the Yeti to a halt on the hardstanding in front of the house. To the side I could see the open garages with their complement of cars. The Jaguar, the BMW, the Porsche and the Mercedes. Conspicuous consumption or what? Typical of a man who thought a sufficiently large dose of money could solve any problem.

Good news, though. If the cars were there, it probably meant their owners were too.

I stepped out of the Yeti and started towards the front door. Then I felt a sudden, crushing pain on the back of my head and the world went black.

# TWENTY-FIVE

I woke to the familiar dream. I was strapped in a car seat, somehow immobilized, and there was no oxygen in what I was breathing. Just the vile smell of petrol. The only difference was that now I also felt a terrible pain at the back of my head.

Oh, and there was one other difference. This wasn't a dream. This was real.

My main thought, the terrible crippling thought was: what will happen to Ben? Will he be able to manage in the harsh world without me?

I tried moving but couldn't. My wrists had been joined together by what felt like plastic plant ties. Just like Kerry's had been.

This wasn't how I'd wanted to go. In fact, I'd never wanted to go. My relentless optimism did not allow such thoughts.

But it didn't seem like I had a lot of choice in the matter, I thought, as consciousness once again slipped away.

The next thing I was aware of was being lifted by strong arms and carried. I was too woozy to know who my rescuer was, but gradually I began to taste air with some nourishment in it. The ghastly metallic fog in my throat was diluted by oxygen. My head throbbed with pain.

I felt myself being laid down on something – a bed, perhaps. As my senses recovered, I realized it was a sofa. The ties had been removed from my wrists.

My eyes had been closed tight against the stinging fumes, but when I opened them, I found myself in the Tallises' sitting room. Jeanette, flawlessly dressed as ever, was sitting in an armchair opposite me. And standing around the sofa were Bruce, Ramiro and Constancia.

I still didn't know which of them had rescued me. Or indeed which had brained me and fixed me in the car with a pipe from the exhaust. I did realize, though, that I was in a potentially very dangerous situation. I closed my eyes and feigned continuing unconsciousness. But I didn't think I'd be able to keep up that pretence for long.

I heard Jeanette's voice asking, 'Has she recovered?'

'She'll live,' said Bruce. It was hard to tell from his tone whether he thought this was good news or bad.

'Why on earth did she come here?' asked Constancia. 'She's just a woman who once helped do some tidying up for Madam.' A bit of an understatement, I thought, but maintained my pose of insensibility.

'Also,' said Bruce icily, 'the woman who discovered Kerry's body in that flat in Portsmouth.'

'That could be just coincidence,' said Jeanette.

Her husband snorted. 'Rather a big coincidence.'

'It is a good question, though. Why does she come here?' asked Ramiro. 'She must be suspicious something is wrong.'

'Something definitely is wrong,' snapped Bruce. 'My daughter's dead.'

'It was going to happen one day,' said Jeanette, a new callousness in her tone. 'No one who uses drugs like she did is going to die in bed, are they? If you're looking for culprits, you should be finding out who was supplying her with drugs towards the end.'

'I've been trying to do that,' said Bruce.

Then why don't you own up, I thought, that it was you. Les recognized you from the photograph. I wasn't sure how much longer I could stop myself from participating in the conversation. I had to remember that somebody in that room had just tried to kill me. Or maybe everyone in that room had conspired to try and kill me. I stayed immobile.

'I still don't know why she come here,' said Ramiro plaintively.

'I do,' said Jeanette. This was a surprise to me and, from the sounds of the others' reactions, to them too. She went on, 'Since I heard she discovered the body, I've done some research on Ellen Curtis.'

'How?'

'I hired a private detective, Bruce. And he told me that she had a husband who committed suicide using the car exhaust method.'

'So?'

'So, she comes here to kill herself by the same method. But, of course, she was saved from doing that. Which will perhaps turn out to have been a pity.'

I did not agree with her on that.

'But why on earth would she have come here to commit suicide?' asked Bruce.

'Because she could not live with the guilt any longer,' his wife replied.

'What guilt?'

'The guilt of having killed Kerry.'

'What on earth makes you think she killed Kerry?'

Bruce's question was a very valid one, and I too would be interested to hear the answer.

Jeanette sounded very composed as she said, 'She was the first one to find the body. Often that person turns out to be the murderer.'

'In crime fiction maybe, Jeanette. Not in the real world.'

I heard Ramiro's voice next. 'I agree with Madam. It would have been better, sir, if you had let her go through with it. With the suicide.'

'I couldn't have done that! I walked past the garage. I heard the engine running. I couldn't just let her die. I'm not in the business of killing people.'

Aren't you? was my silent question.

'Sir, Madam.' It was Constancia. 'I must talk. There have been bad things going on here.'

'That's no worry of yours,' said Jeanette. 'You're shortly going back to Albufeira. Nothing that happens here will ever concern you again.'

'But why are we going back to Albufeira?' Constancia asked.

'To open the bloody restaurant that Ramiro has been going on about ever since you started working here!'

'But why can we open the restaurant? Why do we suddenly have money to open the restaurant?'

'I don't know,' said Jeanette. 'That's not my business.'

And suddenly I saw it. I understood. And I realized there had not been just one man in the photograph I'd sent to Les. There had been two. One in the passenger seat. And one in the driving seat.

Time for me to join the conversation. I sat up, which caused a moment of shock for the other four.

'It is your business, Jeanette,' I said, 'because you have provided the money to buy the restaurant.'

'You're talking nonsense,' she said.

'No, I'm not.'

'No, she's not,' Constancia echoed me.

'What the hell's going on here?' asked Bruce, frustrated by his bewilderment.

'What is going on,' I said calmly, 'is that your wife has been paying Ramiro to do her dirty work.'

'It's not true!' shouted Jeanette.

'Yes, it is.' Constancia backed me up again.

'Ramiro was paid to find Kerry, who by that stage was calling herself "Celeste". He was the one who supplied her with drugs in her last weeks.'

Bruce looked incredulously from me to his butler. 'But why? Why would he do that?'

'Money,' I said. 'We've established that.'

'It is true,' said Constancia. 'I found the heroin and the drug equipment under our bed. First, I think Ramiro has a habit himself. But when I accuse him, no, he says. And he tells me the truth. Like what he is doing is a good thing. Like, when we have the money for the restaurant in Albufeira, all will be happy for the rest of our lives. And I say, no, not with that money. The way you earn that money, it will always be bad money. But Ramiro does not listen to me.'

Bruce had now emerged from his bewilderment. Confusion had been replaced by fury. He turned on Ramiro. 'You! You supplied Kerry with heroin!'

'He did more than that,' said Constancia. Her voice was low with pent-up fury. 'He told me how he got the money. He thinks I will admire him. He thinks I will not tell anyone. Which just shows how little he knows me, how little he has ever known me. You know, he was actually proud of what he'd done.'

'What did he do?' asked Bruce, dangerously quiet.

'He found where Kerry was in Portsmouth. She was calling herself "Celeste" by then, and her drug habit was out of hand. He procured heroin for her. He spent a lot of time around her, watching, waiting for his opportunity. One day he follows her into this flat on the Hargood Estate. It is in a terrible mess, the right place, he thinks. He has with him, prepared, a syringe of pure heroin, not cut with anything. He tells me it is powerful enough to kill someone not used to such strength. He offers it to Kerry in the flat.'

Ramiro was watching his wife, in a state of silent shock. I don't think he had ever heard her talk so much.

'But Kerry will not inject herself,' Constancia went on. 'Something makes her suspicious. Ramiro realizes he will have to force her to do it. She is now very weak, but still she resists. He hits her in the face, subdues her. Then he ties her wrists with plastic ties. Still she resists. He hit her on the head with a chair leg. Then he injects her forcibly and she dies. He removes the plastic ties and leaves her body, *feeling pleased with himself.*' The last words were imbued with a lifetime's rancour, a lifetime of subjugation to an unworthy man.

Before we could stop him, Bruce had rushed across the room and was pummelling the shorter man, blows raining on to his face and chest. The pent-up fury inside him was terrifying to behold.

Eventually, Constancia and I managed to pull the two men apart. Ramiro sank down on to the floor, whimpering, blood pouring from his nose and mouth.

'Let the police deal with him,' I said. 'And while they're at it, they can question him about trying to murder me in the garage.'

Jeanette did not move from her armchair. She just sat there, the picture of middle-class elegance.

Bruce turned on her. 'And you paid him? You paid him to kill Kerry?'

She smiled. A cool, charming smile. 'Well, darling,' she said, 'I had to get your attention somehow.'

# TWENTY-SIX

My throat was still very sore when I got home. Not to mention the wound in the back of my head. I washed the area around it and fixed on a plaster as best I could. I opened another bottle of Merlot and realized what I really wanted to do. I wanted to talk to Oliver about everything that had happened in the previous week. That's one of the worst things about bereavement, and people say it's the same when you lose a partner to dementia – you no longer have someone to process events with. And Oliver could also have seen where to fix the plaster neatly on the back of my head. But he wasn't there. Never would be again.

So, I just sat at the kitchen table and drank wine.

It was all of a piece, I suddenly understood, Jeanette Tallis's behaviour. The problem we had first met over had been prompted by the same motive. She overbought and hoarded clothes in the hope that Bruce would see what she was spending and remonstrate with her. But he, being the man he was, regarded her actions as some kind of validation. He was so rich, his wife could overspend outrageously and he deliberately would not call her to account.

And, in a way, bringing me in had kind of worked, from Jeanette's point of view. It had alerted him to her habit of extravagance, and he had reacted by taking her to the Georges Cinq in Paris. 'Time out for just the two of us,' she had said proudly at the time. She had succeeded. She had his attention.

But, with a man like Bruce Tallis, that was never going to last for long. When I thought about it, there was a similarity between him and Philip Boredean. Both obsessed with their work, and neither fully aware of the effect their behaviour was having on their wives.

So, Jeanette Tallis had resorted to the ultimate way to focus Bruce on her. She would remove what he loved more than her, by having his daughter killed.

No doubt, cushioned by money and belief in the power of money, she thought she would get away with it. I wondered how she would have played her trump card. Would she have been content just to have eliminated the rival to her affections? Or, if Bruce continued to ignore her, might she at some point have admitted to organizing the killing and really got his attention?

I had no means of knowing, but I inclined to the latter view.

Certainly, there was now no possibility that Kerry's murder would go unpunished. As I had, somewhat unsteadily, departed from Lorimers that evening, I had left Bruce Tallis in no doubt that I would tell the police everything I knew. Constancia, appalled by her husband's behaviour, assured her boss that she would do the same.

Bruce, I was sure, would hire the most expensive lawyers available, who would no doubt build up Ramiro's responsibility for the crime, but I didn't think Jeanette could escape scot-free. Somewhere there must be financial records of the dealings between her and her Portuguese 'blunt instrument'.

The whole set-up made me desperately sad. Apart from anything else, the murder was probably unnecessary. Given the trajectory of Kerry Tallis's life, before too long she was likely to have killed herself with an accidental overdose.

Anyway, I did my duty as a good citizen the following morning, the Saturday. Detective Inspector Prendergast came to my home and I gave him the full details of everything I had found out. He was, of course, cagey about how far the official investigations had gone. No doubt their researches would in time have found out Liam Burgess's true identity and tied him to the murder of Nate Ogden. But he didn't reveal how much of what I told him he knew already.

Once I'd talked to Prendergast, I felt exhausted. Traumatized too, I suppose, after the events of the night before. And still with a splitting headache.

Once again, I couldn't settle to anything. I had an instinct to call someone. Not Hilary, though. Nor Ben; I didn't want to spoil his weekend of potential passion. And certainly not Jools or Fleur.

I rang Dodge. His phone must have identified the caller because
he didn't sound at all surly.

'Hi, Dodge,' I said. 'Are you brewing nettle tea?'

'Just this minute,' he said. 'Fancy a cup?'

We drank it outside his living quarters. Even though it was
still April, the weather had decided it couldn't be bothered to
put off summer any longer. We sat at a pallet table on two of his
beautifully made pallet chairs. His seat was plaited orange nylon
rope, mine blue.

'What's with the back of your head?' he asked.

'Someone hit me there.'

He got out of his chair and moved round to look at the wound,
still covered with my inexpertly applied plaster.

'Do you want me to tell you what happened?' I asked.

'No. Not until I've patched you up.'

I shouldn't have been surprised, though I didn't know till then
that Dodge's skills extended to herbal medicine. He went back
inside and returned with a neat box made from recycled panel-
ling. He put it on the table and opened it to reveal a row of glass
bottles, some tubs and dressings. Though obviously I couldn't
see what he was actually doing behind my back, I could see
which treatments he took out of the box.

The one he applied first, which I think was just to cleanse
the wound, stung a bit, but the next seemed to numb that pain
like a local anaesthetic. I could hardly feel the ointment being
applied, was just aware of it being rubbed in. Then Dodge
pressed a pad of something against my skin and fixed it
somehow.

He went back to his chair and his nettle tea. 'Right,' he said,
'who's been beating you up?'

'The butler did it,' I began. And I gave him the whole narrative of the previous week. Needless to say, this was a more
personalized account than the one I had given, in serial form
over the last week, to Detective Inspector Prendergast. Nor did
Dodge interrupt me with supplementary questions.

When I had exhausted both the story and myself, he finally
commented. 'You took a lot of risks.'

'What do you mean? I was desperate to know the truth of
what happened.'

'Maybe. But you were still asking for trouble going to the Tallises' place yesterday.'

'I suppose I was.' The anaesthetic effect of whatever he'd put on the back of my head was wearing off, and the revived ache made me realize just what a risk I had taken.

'Hmm.' There was a silence. Dodge moved his head, as if he was about to look directly at me. At the last moment he lost his nerve. 'If you ever get involved in anything like that again,' he said, '. . . which I hope you don't . . . be sure you take me along with you next time.'

'Thank you, Dodge,' I said, warmed by the offer. 'I will. Incidentally, your mate Les . . .'

'Yes?'

'I might ring him, just to confirm that, in the photo I sent him, it was Ramiro he identified as Kerry's dealer, rather than Bruce.'

'But you know it was, don't you?'

'Yes, must have been.' I havered for a moment. That wasn't why I'd introduced Les's name into the conversation. I went on, 'He's desperately sorry to have let you down . . . over the ReProgramme thing.'

'I know.'

'Is there any chance he could get back on to the counselling training . . .?'

'I'm working on it, Ellen. My argument is that, for a set-up like ReProgramme to black someone after one lapse back into using, well . . . it goes against the whole spirit of the organization.'

'Do you think you will be able to get him back?'

'Quietly confident.'

I knew how much difference that would make to someone in Les's situation. He's one of the good guys, Dodge.

'You want more tea?'

'I'm fine at the moment, thanks.'

'You going to be all right, Ellen?'

'What do you mean?'

'You've been through a lot.'

'I'll be all right, Dodge.'

'When you've processed it.'

'When I've processed it, yes.'

'Some people find that stuff easy.'

'Yes.'

'Lucky them.' Dodge sighed. 'There's a quote from Queen Elizabeth the first on that very subject.'

'Is there?' I was surprised. Not one of his usual sources.

'"They pass best over this world who trip over it quickly; for it is but a bog – if we stop, we sink."'

'True. Funny, I wouldn't have expected that from Queen Elizabeth the first.'

'Trouble is,' said Dodge, 'neither you nor I are very good at doing that, are we – tripping over quickly?'

'No,' I said ruefully. 'We're not.'

I never did hear whether Ricky Brewer was brought to justice. Given his planning in terms of the way he'd got into Hilary's confidence, it was quite possible that he'd planned his escape route with equal efficiency. Maybe, satisfied to have achieved the revenge that he'd always sought, he lived out his life in another country, under yet another identity (probably without a beard). But I doubt whether he lived it out happily. No one who'd written the kind of stuff Ben had found on his laptop could have lived happily.

Bad news on the Ashleigh front, though. The inevitable happened. Another shouting match with one of her neighbours led to the police being called to the block. Ashleigh was found to be using again. I'll do what I can, so will the social workers, but I don't think we'll be able to prevent Zak from being taken into care. And the downward spiral will start all over again, just as it had with Ricky Brewer.

Sometimes, with my clients, I almost scream with frustration about how little I can do.

Ben was good about sending texts and I was delighted to receive one on the Saturday afternoon to say he wouldn't be back till Sunday evening. Maybe this relationship with Tracey will work out. I hope so. The test will come the first time she sees him really depressed. If they can survive that, the prospects are good. And I know he will get depressed again. He may get better, but he'll never be completely cured. He has to live with that, and I have to live with the resultant anxiety.

Something I did do on the Saturday was go to the cupboard under the stairs and take out one of the cartoons I'd had framed for Oliver's forty-third birthday. I hung it up in the hall. I have come that far.

I didn't hear from Jools in the week after she'd been down for Sunday lunch, but that's not unusual. I'm sure she's fine.

But of course, I did hear from my mother and, would you believe, she had heard from Jools. On the Saturday afternoon Fleur rang, inviting me to lunch at Goodwood with her the following day. Kenneth, needless to say, would be playing golf.

For a moment I wondered if Fleur Bonnier could make up a threesome of neglected wives. Like Hilary, like Jeanette, a third one suffering from her husband's inattention . . .?

But the minute I saw her on the Sunday, I knew she didn't fit the template. Her self-esteem was far too strong. I have a sneaking admiration for the way it has kept her buoyant through a series of reversals that might have downed a lesser woman. It just never occurs to her that she could be in the wrong.

I'd arranged taxis both ways to Goodwood, so I could drink with impunity. Drink and listen. My mother, annoying though she can frequently be, is a good raconteur. In her telling of it, she can dress up the dullest of events into something sparkling. And she spent most of the lunch dressing up the events of her week – basically a couple of lunches and a few phone calls to showbiz friends – into a compelling narrative.

When we'd ordered coffee, she paused for breath. 'Anyway, darling, how's your week been?'

'Oh, usual stuff,' I replied. 'Not a lot.'

'And it's back to the boring old cleaning tomorrow, is it, Ellen?'

'That's right, Fleur,' I said. 'Back to the boring old cleaning.'